Man-to-Man

Man-to-Man

Bill Swan

James Lorimer & Company Ltd., Publishers
Toronto

James Lorimer & Company Ltd. acknowledges the support of the Ontario
Arts Council. We acknowledge the support of the Government of Canada
through the Book Publishing Industry Development Program (BPIDP)
for our publishing activities. We acknowledge the support of the Canada
Council for the Arts for our publishing program. We acknowledge the
support of the Government of Ontario through the Ontario Media
Development Corporation's Ontario Book Initiative.

Cover illustration: Greg Ruhl

The Canada Council | Le Conseil des Arts
for the Arts | du Canada

ONTARIO ARTS COUNCIL
CONSEIL DES ARTS DE L'ONTARIO

Library and Archives Canada Cataloguing in Publication

Swan, Bill, 1939-
    Man-to-man / Bill Swan.

 (Sports stories)
 ISBN 978-1-55277-443-4 (bound).--ISBN 978-1-55277-442-7 (pbk.)

    I. Title. II. Series: Sports stories

PS8587.W338T69 2009   jC813'.54   C2009-901677-X

James Lorimer & Co. Ltd.,	Distributed in the United States by:
Publishers	Orca Book Publishers
317 Adelaide Street West,	P.O. Box 468
Suite 1002	Custer, WA USA
Toronto, Ontario	98240-0468
M5V 1P9	
www.lorimer.ca	

Printed and bound in Canada.

CONTENTS

For Jack, Hannah, Duncan and Quinlan.

Special thanks to Kat, who always proves the value of copy editors; and to my daughter, Gavy, who proofread the final draft and showed the value of proofreaders.

1 On the Bench

From the players' bench, Michael Reilly leaned forward to watch his lacrosse team in action at the far end of a hockey rink with no ice.

To do so he had to lean forward on his lacrosse stick, and balance himself on his tip-toes. Even then, his eyes just cleared the boards. He had seen the pictures his mother had taken of him sitting on the bench: two eyes, and a helmet above the boards.

He was the shortest kid on his team.

The youngest kid on his team.

"Keep hanging in there, Michael," Coach Vickers said, tapping him lightly on the helmet.

Their team, the Clarington Thunder, trailed the Six Nations Warriors 5–4. It was the second of four games the team would play in the Ontario Provincial Lacrosse Championships — five if they made it to the semifinals, six if they played the finals. But the Warriors were fast, tough, and, as they loved to remind everybody, last year's champions.

It was the second period. Coach Vickers paced behind the players. He chewed gum loudly. From time to time he glanced up at the clock on the scoreboard. "Soon, Michael. Soon," he said, his eyes focused on the play. "You'll get some time out there."

Michael had been proud to earn a spot on the team. The Thunder was a team selected from the top two players from each team in the Clarington house league. In league games, Michael had played a lot. But it didn't take long before the pride of being chosen for Thunder had begun to leak out of him like air from a punctured bicycle tire. It was halfway through the second game of the provincial championship tournament, and Michael hadn't played even one shift.

Vince Bell jabbed him with an elbow. "Bencher." He said it with a sneer. Michael knew that, in Vince's eyes, Michael just was not part of the team. In house-league games, Michael's lacrosse skills rivalled most of the other players on the team. But in house-league games, Coach Vickers was Vince's coach, not Michael's.

Michael tried to ignore Vince. He could barely see his team's goal at the far end. There, the only Thunder player who had been on Michael's house-league team, goalie Duncan Quinn, blocked a shot and scooped the ball. That was the signal for the line change. The coach clacked the bolt on the bench door to tell the players on the floor to return to the bench in a shift change.

Standing on toes, and peeking in and around taller players, Michael could see Jordan Shelby at the far end untangle himself from a Warrior he had checked in the last play.

Coach Vickers continued clicking the bolt, yelling, "Hurryhurryhurry!" Vince pushed by the coach and into the game just as Jason Moore came off.

Michael watched Vince streak across the floor, take a long pass, and head toward the Warriors goal, picking up speed as he ran. Two Warriors, one on each side of Vince, repeatedly hit him with cross-checks.

Ignoring them, Vince bulled his way toward the goal, holding his lacrosse stick high and away. The two defenders continued to hack at him, their sticks held firmly in both hands, trying to dislodge the ball. Michael saw Vince look around for a teammate to pass to. But the line change had not been completed. Vince was alone.

Vince took one hard check that put him off balance. As he fell, he flicked a quick shot low and hard at the Warriors goal. But the Warriors goalie read the shot and easily scooped up the ball. Immediately players from both teams reversed direction and headed down the arena for the Thunder goal. The Warriors goalie handed off to his right corner, who then led the attack. Jack Hannah, playing left crease for the Thunder, tried blocking the attacker's path.

Michael glanced at the shot clock. As the team in

possession of the ball, the Warriors had only thirty seconds to shoot on goal.

Both teams now headed toward the Thunder goal, where the Thunder players put up a defensive block around the net. The Warriors passed the ball quickly around the outside, looking for an opening.

Michael always thought this kind of attack looked like a power play in hockey. He tried to keep his eye on the ball from the bench, but his taller teammates kept leaning forward, blocking his view.

A roar rose from the crowd — spectators shouted, pointing to the far corner. Michael leaned farther forward, slipping off the bench and standing on his toes to look down the boards. Duncan, thick and heavy in his goalie pads, gestured to the corner but kept his eyes on the ball.

By leaning to his left and tilting his head to the right, Michael could make out what everyone was pointing and staring at. A crumpled figure lay on the floor near the boards by the corner.

"Look, Coach. Jordan's hurt!" Michael said. Jordan was Michael's best friend on the team. He and Duncan were house-league teammates, but Jordan was in Michael's class at school and lived only one street over from him.

The parents in the stands continued to yell. "Come on, ref," one voice broke through. "He's hurt. Use your whistle."

Play continued. The referee glanced once to the corner, then at the Thunder bench, but no whistle sounded. Michael couldn't see clearly. He knew the rules allowed the ref to stop play if he thought an injury was serious. Otherwise, the play continued until a play stoppage or possession change.

"Come on, ref! You're missing a good game!" the same loud voice yelled from the stands.

Michael recognized that voice. It was Mr. Shelby, Jordan's father. Everyone called him Leather Lungs. He was always on top of referees. "Open yer eyes!" Mr. Shelby shouted.

Michael watched Jordan struggle to his knees before his vision was blocked again.

"Stay on it! Stay on it!" yelled Coach Vickers, trying to keep the team focused. No whistle had sounded, so the game was continuing on.

The Warriors passed the ball deftly — point to left corner, left crease, point, right corner. Their ball-handling was legendary. With one Thunder defender injured, they pressed the advantage to add to their one-goal lead.

Abrams, the tall lanky point for the Warriors, took a pass in the centre between the two faceoff circles. He charged straight in. He was checked by two defending Thunder players, but spun between them. Abrams got off a hard overhead shot that sizzled cleanly into the top left corner of the goal over Duncan's right shoulder.

6–4.

Immediately, the ref gestured to the Thunder bench to send a trainer to look after the injured player.

With one foot on the boards, Michael could see Jordan get to his feet. Jordan leaned on both knees and shook his head.

"Get down, Reilly," said the coach. "Let's make some room for Jordan."

The team trainer — Dylan Shea's father — helped Jordan through the door to the players bench and sat him on a corner seat. He removed Jordan's helmet and peered into his eyes.

"You okay?" he asked.

Jordan smiled weakly. "You asked me that before. I'm fine."

"He says he's fine," announced Mr. Shea.

"I heard," said Coach Vickers. "But *is* he fine?"

"He looks okay. But he had his bell rung. Maybe he should sit out a shift or two."

Coach Vickers looked at Jordan. "Okay. We'll see how you feel." Over his shoulder he said to Michael, "Reilly, be ready. We may need you for a shift or two to replace Jordan's speed."

Michael held his stick firmly. He did want to play a shift. He didn't want Jordan being hurt as the reason for his chance, but there was nothing he could do about that. "I'm ready," he said.

But it turned out that Jordan was back out on the

floor before the end of the period, and Michael didn't get to play in his place at all.

Maybe in the third period, thought Michael.

2 Disputed Call

"Hang in there, Michael," the coach said halfway through the third period. "You'll get a chance to play. This tournament isn't over yet."

The way he said it did not give Michael much hope. Brandon Henderson and Vince had both been double-shifted twice while Michael sat on the bench.

In the stands, Jordan's father yelled, "Ooogga, Ooogga, Ooogga!"

And other parents replied, "Boogga, Boogga, Boogga!"

Together: "Thunder, Thunder, Thunder!"

Then they all stamped their feet on the floor, or kicked against the outside of the boards to make the sound of rolling thunder.

Duncan grabbed the ball in his crease. He hit Vince with a long pass, Vince snapped a quick pass to Walt Wilson, the point, as he crossed centre.

A Warrior hit Vince hard with a two-handed cross

check on the shoulder, then a second just above his waist. The Warrior tripped, his stick raking Vince along the side of the knee.

Even from the bench, the pain on Vince's face was clear. While the Warriors took over possession, Vince hobbled to the bench with a Terry Fox hop-skip. Coach Vickers patted Michael on the helmet. Twice.

"Get out there!" he said.

Michael raced onto the floor.

Walt ran the ball toward centre, flicked a pass to Michael, who by now had reached full speed. Only one Warrior — Abrams, their star player — was anywhere near him.

Michael reached high, pulled in the pass, and dug even deeper for speed.

The Warrior right corner, caught counting the house, steamed in from the boards to Michael's right. Ahead, Michael could see the goalie moving up high on the crease. Like most goalies this one was short, broad, and padded out like a weightlifter on a sugar diet. He left little space to shoot at.

Five more strides, Michael thought. Five strides and he would be in a good shooting position. He didn't make it. Abrams pummelled him with cross-checks that shoved him forward and knocked him off balance, for one, two, wobbly strides before he skidded belly-down on the concrete floor. Face to the floor, Michael whacked at the ball as it rolled out of his stick. He watched it dribble weakly before being scooped up by the goalie.

Abrams gave Michael one more crack with his stick that the ref couldn't see, and turned away.

Michael scrambled to his feet, stumbling twice. The play had already turned past centre. The Warriors were closing in on the Thunder goal.

Michael sprinted toward the action. From the bench came the familiar *clack-clack-clack* of the lock bolt — line change.

Michael reluctantly looked at the bench. He saw the coach gesturing to him, and Brad ready to come on.

Brad bolted from the opposite door as soon as Michael stepped into the exchange zone. Before he even got to his familiar spot on the bench, a cheer came from the Warriors bench and half the crowd rose.

The Warriors had scored.

The coach uttered a word that wasn't really a word — a kind of a grunt with a grimace, a sound that, had it been a word, would have been a very bad one.

"Sorry," Michael said to no one in particular. No one seemed to hear.

When the crowd had settled down and play had resumed, the coach came over and stood behind Michael.

"Don't sweat it," he said. "You'll do better next time."

From the bench, Michael watched as Jordan

scooped the loose ball at centre, pivoted around two defenders, and sped in on goal.

Pummelled from behind, Jordan sank to his knees. But he got a quick shot away that the Warriors goalie blocked easily.

Still caught in the momentum of the last cross-check, Jordan continued his lunge toward the goal. The ball bounced once in front of him, high. Still off-balance, he fell into the crease, whacking the ball out of the air with his stick before colliding with the goalie in a tangled heap of legs in the crease. Michael admired Jordan's hand-eye coordination that enabled him to hit a ball in the air like that. But Vince had one foot in the crease.

When the Thunder bench exploded in celebration, Michael kept his seat. He waited to see how the ref would call this one — a clear crease violation.

The crowd roared, half cheering, half protesting, before settling into a stunned silence that was quickly punctuated by the ref's whistle.

The ref's signal was clear — arms out and palms flat. Crease violation. No goal.

The crowd exhaled, then moaned. The Warriors fans yelled enthusiastically. Then, one loud, boisterous voice broke through.

"They feeding you Firewater, Ref?"

All eyes searched the arena for the source of the offensive remark. Michael thought the crowd seemed to fidget in embarrassment. Then attention swung back to the ref. He was scanning the crowd with laser eyes, looking for the biggest mouth in the house.

The same voice echoed again from the rafters. "Open yer eyes, Chief. You're missing a good game."

It was Mr. Shelby. Michael could see him, with his red hair and thick moustache, standing at the third tier with his back to the wall, arms folded across his chest.

The ref used the shocked silence that filled the arena to regain control. He aimed one finger at Mr. Shelby, then sharply at the arena door. Michael felt embarrassed for Jordan.

"What, me?!" asked Mr. Shelby, looking up and down the line of spectators as though someone else had been shouting insults at the ref. "You gotta be kidding!"

The ref stood at the centre of the box now, pointing to the door. His whistle sounded sharply. "The game resumes when you are gone," he said, his loud voice almost lost in the echoes of the rink.

Michael couldn't believe that this man who was causing so much trouble was the same man who bought Michael and Jordan ice cream after hot summer games. He watched Mr. Shelby stomp toward the exit.

Mr. Shelby mumbled and grumbled as he went, trying his best to slam the door on his way out. Instead, the hydraulic closer hissed at him as he left.

A few last seconds of silence followed before the ref blasted his whistle for the faceoff to resume play.

3 Toughing It Out

The provincials of the Ontario Lacrosse League were held each year in the town of Whitby during the first two weeks in August. It was Michael's first year at the provincials. He was amazed at how big the event was. Games were scheduled for the Vipond Arena in Brooklin and one of the six arenas at Iroquois Park. Michael stayed with his mother and sister in a hotel near the expressway, close to all the games.

After the game, Michael carried his equipment out to the lobby. Most of his teammates had hurried out to meet up with their parents.

Michael saw that Mr. Shelby had waited for the game to end. He was trying to rumple Jordan's hair. Jordan kept pulling away.

"It was that one bad call," he was saying. "No, make that two bad calls. Maybe three. Curse that ref. That goal of yours should have counted, it really should. That was the victory right there. You weren't in the crease. You didn't touch the guy. And the way he took you into the boards. Yeesh."

He turned to Michael. "Your dad here today?"

Michael shrugged.

"Too bad," said Mr. Shelby. "That must be hard for him, missing your games and all."

It had never occurred to Michael that his father might feel one way or the other about watching him play. For as long as Michael could remember, his father had spent all his time writing and rewriting his book.

"Well, maybe he'll be done writing that book before next year," said Mr. Shelby. "Either that, or some day he's going to wake up and smell the dressing room. By then you'll be playing pro for the Rock, ha, ha."

Michael didn't think it was funny, but laughed anyway. He had seen Toronto's professional lacrosse team on TV, and some of his teammates had even been to games. Sure, Michael daydreamed of playing for the Rock. But what he really, really wanted was a regular shift in the provincials with the Thunder.

"But this is a rough game," Mr. Shelby continued. "You've got to be able to take some punishment, to suck it up. You do that and you'll spend more time in the game. Like Jordan here. If he couldn't take a hit, his speed wouldn't count for much. You saw how he shook it off and got back in the game." He reached over again to rumple Jordan's hair. Jordan pulled away.

Everybody kept telling Michael the same thing:

suck it up, take the hit, be tough. But nobody ever told him what being tough really meant, aside from not falling down when bigger players checked you.

Mr. Shelby turned to Jordan and said, "That guy hit you from behind. That's for sure. And that last goal should have counted."

"That's all right, Dad," Jordan said. "I was in the crease."

"Okay, okay," said Mr. Shelby. "You're fairer than I am. Maybe too fair. What did I do wrong?" he chuckled. He didn't wait for an answer. "But you guys are lucky. Do you know who was watching this game?" His voice was loud enough to carry to the rest of the players standing around. "Scotty Martin, that's who."

The silent faces waited for more information.

"You don't know who Scotty Martin is? How about you, Mr. Einstein, reader of the Wikken Encyclopedia?" He looked at Michael.

"It's Wikipedia, Dad," said Jordan.

"Whatever. Tell them who Scotty Martin is, Michael."

"He's the coach of the Canadian National team," said Michael cautiously. He hated the way everyone was straining to catch his words.

"Do say!"

"And a hall-of-fame player. A member of the Brooklin Redmen, the 1987 Mann Cup champions."

"That's right, kid." Mr. Shelby turned back to his

son. "Too bad that a bad call got in your way of stardom. That Six Nations team plays a dirty game, and they have that ref on their side. If he lets those guys get away with murder and scalping like that, somebody's going to get hurt."

Jordan made a face that his father didn't see. Michael looked around frantically, and was relieved to see his mother appear from a crowd near the concession stand.

"Well, hello, all you beautiful people!" said Mrs. Reilly, sweeping her arms wide to encompass the world. "What a great game! You guys played just awesome. Did you win?"

Michael couldn't believe how clueless his mother was. Was she watching the game at all? "We lost 6–4," he explained. "But I did get to play. Did you see it? One shift."

"Get away with you! You didn't! You're kidding, right? Well, we'll have to tell your grandparents all about that."

"There's not much to tell," said Michael. "One shift."

"Didn't you see the game, Mrs. Reilly?" Mr. Shelby asked. "They put Michael, Mr. Lawyer here into the game after Jordan got hurt. And he almost got a shot on goal."

Michael winced. He hated being called Mr. Lawyer. He didn't want to be a lawyer. He wanted to be a lacrosse player.

"I'm really sorry I missed that," she said. "I had to take Rebekah to the washroom through most of the third period." Rebekah, seven years old and blonde, bounced up and down beside her mother.

"I just got back as you were leaving," she said to Mr. Shelby. "What happened there, at the end?"

Mr. Shelby put his hands on his hips so his elbows stuck out. "I got kicked out of game, can you believe that?"

"Can they do that to a spectator?"

"You'd think that at the provincials they would get impartial referees. That, after they hammered Jordan into the boards. Did you see that part? He could have been really seriously hurt. And when he did get back into the game they shoved him into the goal crease when he scored."

"Dad," said Jordan, pleading.

"Who did this?" asked Mrs. Reilly.

"I dunno who. One of the Warriors."

"But, Dad," Jordan broke in, "nobody hit me on the head. I got checked and stumbled. It knocked the wind out of me."

"Look, you were half stunned there for several minutes. You don't go down like that from a cross-check. And those guys are masters at cheap shots."

Michael thought the Warriors were just very good lacrosse players, but he wasn't going to say anything.

Jordan already looked miserable enough.

Rebekah stopped bouncing and squeezed up to her mother, her face like a little moonbeam. "Can we get my Princess Ponies?" she asked.

Rebekah had brought a carrying case full of pink toys, including ponies and carriages and ballerinas with hair to their elbows, to every lacrosse game Michael had ever played. She played with them during the game.

"You didn't leave them in the arena, did you?" asked her mother.

Rebekah nodded her head vigorously. She grabbed her mother's hand in both of hers and leaned backward, pulling. "Get my dolls," she said.

"Some day you're going to leave your dolls and when you get back they will be gone," said Mrs. Reilly. "We really must make sure we gather them up each time." But she allowed herself to be pulled back to the arena.

Several members of the Warriors walked by, carrying sticks and equipment bags.

"Looks like they're on the war path," said Mr. Shelby.

"Don't, Dad," pleaded Jordan.

"Hey, they only beat you because of a homer ref," said Mr. Shelby. "Your goal should have counted. That guy should have got a penalty, too."

As if mentioning him conjured him out of thin air,

the referee from the Warrior–Thunder game walked by. With him was an older man with short blond hair. The ref gave Mr. Shelby a puzzled look, as if trying to place him.

"Well, if it isn't Blind Man's Bluff," said Mr. Shelby in that booming voice again. "Want the number of an optometrist?" He held out his glasses.

"Dad," said Jordan.

"That's okay, son. If these guys are as deaf as they are blind, they didn't hear that." He turned toward the back of the departing referee. "Right?" His voice got even louder as he called after the two men. "What about your friend, ref? Is he blind, too?"

The ref started to turn back. The older man — not that much older, perhaps the age of Michael's father — reached out a hand and grabbed the ref's elbow.

Several players from the Warrior's team and their coach pushed through the door from the dressing room. They were talking and laughing among themselves. The coach spotted Jordan and Michael and made his way over.

"You okay?" he said to Jordan. "You went down pretty hard there. Head injuries can be nasty."

Mr. Shelby turned to the coach.

"Yeah, he's okay. It happens. He's tough. What is it to you?"

"I saw him go down," said the Warriors coach, ignoring Mr. Shelby's attitude. "It was a stumble at full speed, and he smacked his shoulder pretty good. There was head contact, too, likely. You might want to have both him and his helmet checked out. Just in case."

"Yeah, but who hit him?" asked Mr. Shelby.

"Hit him? Nobody hit him. There wasn't anybody near him. He stumbled into the boards. Nasty. It happens, not often, but it happens." He patted Jordan on the back. "Good luck in your other games," he said. "Maybe we'll see you guys in the finals. It'd be a tough game for both teams." He walked out of the arena into the hot August sun outside without waiting for Mr. Shelby to answer.

A few members of the Thunder shuffled up, some with parents in tow. Rebekah and her mother returned carrying an armful-and-a-half of pink ponies and dolls.

"How about a dog and a pop?" Mrs. Reilly asked Michael. "The rest of you guys heading out?"

"Sounds good to me," said Mr. Shelby. "How about you, Jordan? Think you've worked up an appetite?"

Jordan smiled wanly. His gaze turned glassy. Suddenly, all Michael could see was the whites of his eyes.

Jordan's knees buckled first. Then he collapsed in a heap over his equipment bag.

4 Michael's Chance

Early the next morning the Thunder met in the dressing room. Their third game of the tournament would be against the Clarington Green Gaels.

Michael dumped his equipment on the dressing-room floor. He started dressing for the game. He put on the shoulder pads, rib pads, arm guards and jock — all would provide the protection he knew he would need — if he played. *Surely*, he thought, *this time I will get a chance.* He sat on the bench with his stick and gloves in one hand and his helmet on his lap.

"Listen up, everybody," said Coach Vickers as he entered the dressing room. "We have another big game today. Maybe our biggest game of the tournament. We've lost one already. This team, the Gaels, beat the Warriors. Now it's our turn to beat the Gaels so all three teams will be tied in the standings."

"Yeah, yeah," some team members mumbled. Michael wondered if they believed that they could beat the Gaels. He wondered if the coach believed it. Like most of the Thunder, Michael had tried out for the Gaels and hadn't made the team.

"Okay, guys. This game we're going to be without Jordan. Most of you know that he collapsed after last game. Right now he's at the hospital. They're checking him out."

"Is he hurt bad?" asked Duncan. "Is he going to be okay?"

"That's why they're examining him. His father is with him, and he promised to let me know as soon as he heard anything."

"Those guys hit him from behind," said Vince, scowling. "And then the ref called it no goal."

"Birty duggers," said Duncan. Sometimes he mixed up his words.

The coach locked eyes with each player in no particular order but missing no one. He held up a hand. "I do not want to hear talk like that. Nobody saw him get hit. The coach on the Warriors said he just stumbled."

"Yeah, that's what he would say," said Vince. "The Warriors should have to pay for it."

"As I said, nobody saw him get hit," repeated the coach. "Whatever happened was part of the last game. We can't let that take us out of this game coming up. To make it to the playoffs, we have to beat the Gaels."

The team remained silent for a few seconds.

"Okay, let's move on," continued the coach. "The Gaels were finalists last year. They think they're the number-one rep team for Clarington. They are fast and skilled, and they think the Cup belongs to them. They are undefeated. They will want to stay undefeated. But I ask you: do they deserve it?"

"No," called a few players.

"Now did that sound like it came from a team that does deserves to win the championship? I'm going to ask again: Do the Gaels deserve to be champions?"

"No!" shouted the team in chorus.

"Again, do the Gaels deserve to be champs?"

"No!"

"Again!"

"NO!"

"Who deserves to be champs?"

"Thunder!" roared the team. They all stamped their feet and battered the butt ends of their sticks on the floor or bench or whatever was handy.

"Who deserves to be champs?"

"Thunder!" roared the team again, even louder.

"Who deserves to be champs?"

"Thunder!"

"Louder!"

"THUNDER!"

Dressed, fit, and supercharged, the Thunder hit the box running.

After a short warm-up, Michael headed for his

usual spot in the middle of the bench. There he would not interfere with players going on and off the floor.

He was surprised when Coach Vickers tapped him on the shoulder. "With Jordan not here, we're going to need you on a regular shift, Michael," he said. "You'll be out there with Vince and Walt. Now let's see you use those legs, and show the rest of the team what little guys can do."

***

By the time Michael got to play his first shift, the Green Gaels were ahead 1–0.

As he left the players bench, the coach said to him, "They're breaking fast, Michael. Keep on them. Use your size."

Michael smirked at that. His size. Sure.

The Thunder was in possession, but the Gaels were confident enough to attempt a line change. Duncan had scooped the ball in front of his own crease, and was firing a pass to Brandon coming off the bench. Brandon whipped the ball to Jack, who did a solo rush at the Gaels goal. He broke in past the surprised Gaels defenders and fired a hard shot from outside the face-off circle to the left of the goal.

The Gael goalie hardly saw the shot, but it hit him in his padded midsection. He scooped up the rebound and sent a long pass to a teammate. The Thunder were caught with an incomplete line change and players out of position.

Michael was one of the Thunder on the floor. He turned to see what seemed to be the whole Gael team coming hard down the near side. He tried to position himself between the player with the ball and his own goal. Michael stuck to the ball carrier, man on man, pushing and badgering him with cross-checks, spinning when he spun, running when he ran, twisting, shoving, doing anything he could to keep the ball away from in front of the Thunder goal.

Despite his efforts, the Gael flipped a quick pass. He spun in a three-quarters turn coming straight in on goal, and took a return pass, leaving Michael going the wrong way.

Without taking time to think, Michael responded. He took two steps sideways. He whacked twice at the player's stick and cross checked vigorously.

Behind him, he heard Duncan yell. "The pass! Watch the pass!"

Michael shifted to cover the free player moving in on goal. He planted himself in the player's path. But the player came anyway, nabbing the ball out of the air above Michael's head, spinning around Michael before he could move. With the ball in the webbing, he lifted his stick behind his head, preparing for a shot on goal.

Now behind the attacker, Michael turned and

lunged, swiping at the attacker's stick. He caught the webbing just enough to tip the shot. Instead of flying hard to the net, the ball dropped and bounced at the attacker's feet.

Michael reached to recover it. An elbow caught his shoulder. He tripped on someone's ankle and found himself on his back. Above and around him players from both teams scrambled for the ball.

Michael reached out to scoop up the bouncing ball. A stray stick struck his shin.

The loose ball bounced twice, as four players reached for it. Everybody tried to grab the ball. Still on his knees amid the legs, arms, and sticks, Michael got it — and instantly became a target. He was pummelled from one side, then the other. He twisted and turned, trying to get to his feet. To lose the ball in front of his own goal could be a disaster. He had to get control of the situation.

Struggling desperately, Michael gained enough space to turn and fire the ball back toward his own goal. Duncan grabbed the ball as it bounced by the far goalpost.

Goalie possession gave Duncan five seconds with the ball — enough time for the team to start moving down the box.

Michael regained his balance and headed down the left boards. From the corner of his eye he saw Vince pick up Duncan's clearing pass on the far side. Vince roared up the right boards, dogged left, and passed to Jack, the point, who had moved down the centre.

As quickly as the Thunder had struck, the Gaels had regrouped. Four of their players had made it back to their side. Jack slowed as he approached the wall of defenders in front of the Gaels goal.

Michael continued his race down the right side, going deep into the left of the goal. Jack hit him with a high pass. Now the defenders turned to Michael, pushing and checking to keep the Thunder away from that dangerous territory in front of the goal.

Michael trotted into the corner, nursed the ball in his racket, and glanced at the shot clock. Ten seconds for the Thunder to attempt a shot on goal or lose possession.

The wall of defenders looked invincible.

Eight seconds.

Michael couldn't find any of his teammates in a decent shooting angle. Determined, he raced from the corner straight into the hot spot in front of the goal — right into the middle of the throng of Gaels defenders.

He pulled his stick back to shoot.

Two cross-checks, a body check, and trip all hit Michael at the same time. He spun twice, grimaced at the pain in his shin, and kissed the floor hard.

The shot bounced off one, two defenders. A Gaels player grabbed the ball and lowered his head to sprint full speed toward the Thunder goal.

5 Back to the Bench

"Smart move, Reilly," said Coach Vickers, eyeing the careful way Michael was moving. "You almost caught them flat. Now all we have to do is put more muscle in your breakfast cereal."

Michael had made it back to the bench, nursing the tender spot on his ribs where a cross-check had caught him under his pads. "It kind of hurts," Michael said, still panting.

"We'll look at it later," said Coach Vickers. "That's just the Gaels showing that they respect you. Good effort. But next time, stay on your feet."

As the game progressed, Michael kept his eyes on the Gaels. Their number 10, Powless, had a combination of speed and skilled moves that made him hard to catch. He scored three of the five Gaels goals by half way through the last period.

With less than three minutes to go, Walt tied the score on his second goal of the game for the Thunder.

5–5.

The clock ticked down.

The helmet on Michael's head felt like a portable oven. The crowd, mostly parents with a few kid sisters, cooled off by fanning themselves and shouting loudly at the ref. Some praised good efforts, as the coach had suggested.

"Good move, Walt, good move."

"Way to go, Duncan!" That was a loud, deep voice that could only be a father.

Sometimes, the shouts from the stands made no sense. "Get 'im, Rob, get 'im!" As though the defender didn't know enough to stop an attacker.

And "Run! Run! Run!" *What else*, Michael thought, *would you do playing lacrosse?*

And the old hockey yell — "Holy Moly, what a goalie!"— whenever either goalie made a good save.

One minute to go. One of the Gaels swiped at the ball and missed, knocking it into the stands.

The Thunder was awarded possession.

Still 5–5.

Coach Vickers called for a time out. The team gathered around the bench. "We need this win," he said.

He paused. The arena buzzed.

"We have one minute. Keep an eye on the shot clock. These guys know that a tie will knock us out of the finals, so they'll try for possession with thirty seconds left to kill our chances.

"On defence, when they have the ball, we need man-to-man coverage here. Vince, cover Powless so close you could share a jock strap. He's got lots of moves, but you've got just as many. And on a change-over he's slow to get back. Use that.

"Walt, keep so close to number twelve that he thinks you're his prom date."

"The rest of you need to stick to your positions, particularly on defence. Michael, I'm going to keep you out there because we need your speed. They won't expect that. Keep your wheels oiled. Play out toward centre and look for a long pass. That will pull one of their corners out of position. We need to press hard and fast. We need a shot as quickly as possible now, so if they get possession we'll still have one more chance."

Michael did the math in his head. It's hard to score without possession, but it's almost as hard to score if you rush a shot. "But —" he began.

The coach answered Michael's question before he even expressed it. "If we shoot and lose possession, we'll try to regain possession. The last thing we want is to use up thirty seconds of possession and hand the ball to the Gaels. They could play keep-away for thirty seconds, and we would be dead."

A cluster of other helmets nodded.

"Okay, time's up. Let's get that goal."

The players returned to the box. The clock showed

less than a minute left in the game, with 25 seconds on the Thunder shot clock.

Vince held possession for the Thunder. He trotted up the box into the attack zone. Twenty seconds left on the shot clock.

The Gaels had formed a tight pattern in front of their goal. Vince faded hard to his right, then flung the ball back to Walt, across to Zak Mathers.

Michael went deep into the right corner and signalled for a pass. He took the ball. Immediately, the Gaels shifted to him. Running hard, Michael headed straight out of the corner toward the hot spot in front of the goal.

They want tough? he thought. *Here's tough.*

Two Gaels defenders made a wall he could not go through. But if it took two to make a wall, that meant someone else on the Thunder was free of a check. Michael took a heavy cross-checking shove, and passed back to Walt, who passed across to Vince in front of the goal.

With ten seconds left on the shot clock, Vince fired a shot hard and high at the goal.

Missed.

The Gaels regained possession with forty seconds left in the game.

Michael watched as Vince went after the ball carrier, pushing with a hearty two-handed cross-check into his waist. The Gaels player stumbled.

Vince hit his opponent once more. As the player fell, Vince checked repeatedly on his stick, trying to dislodge the ball from the webbing. *Whack! Whack!* The Gaels player spun to keep away from him, but Vince stayed with him, hands firmly on his stick, elbows bent — shove, shove.

Michael trotted meekly behind the action.

The ball carrier began to dodge and weave, bend over, swivel. But Vince followed his body movements to stay between the ball possession and his own goal.

Vince badgered the ball carrier, pushing, shoving, checking. But the Gaels player got a pass away and his team moved toward the Thunder goal.

As instructed by the coach, Michael hung back near centre. His check stayed nearby, afraid to join his team in the assault on the Thunder goal in case of a turnover.

The rest of the Thunder closed ranks in a box formation in front of Duncan. The Gaels passed once, twice, and got the ball to Powless in the hot spot directly in front of the goal. Powless fired a shot high, hard, and handsome — and missed the goal. The ball bounced out toward the left boards. The Gaels left corner recovered the ball and was ready to fire it back at the goal, but the shot clock sounded.

Change of possession: Thunder in control.

Duncan took possession and passed quickly to Vince. Vince heaved the ball down court to Michael, who was heading full-speed into the attack zone.

As soon as Michael caught the pass just over the centre zone, an opponent was on him. Michael ducked and spun, but his moves to avoid his check caused the ball to roll from his stick into the corner to the left of the Gaels goal.

Now he had two players to beat. He sprinted to the corner. The Gaels goalie started for the corner, and got halfway to the ball before he realized he might not beat Michael to it. With a defender half a step behind him, Michael reached the ball first.

Instead of picking up the ball, Michael banged at it, sending it bouncing off the boards. It rolled out in front of the Gaels goal.

Vince had followed the play in. He scooped the ball in full flight, and brought his stick up and over in one motion, depositing the ball neatly into the top right corner.

The score was 6–5 for the Thunder. Twenty seconds were left in the game.

Coach Vickers waved Michael to the bench.

"Good work, Michael, " he said. "That was a smart play. But now we need some muscle out there to hold that lead." Zak jogged across the floor to take up his position.

In the faceoff, Vince lost possession. The Gaels struck hard and fast. Their goalie raced to the bench for an extra attacker, and the Gaels closed in on the

Thunder goal.

Michael didn't bother to take a seat on the bench. He stood by the gate, working hard to see around the sea of arms and legs and sticks that blocked his vision of the ball handlers, as Duncan bobbed and weaved in his net. The Gaels probed hard, searching for a weakness, for an opening, for a scoring shot.

The Thunder held them. They pushed and shoved, checking Gaels whether ball carrier or not, always making sure to keep between the ball and the goal.

Then Powless broke through. He swerved once around Vince, faked Walt, and from six metres out fired an overhead shot too fast for Michael to follow.

Twang! The shot echoed off Duncan's face mask and the ball flew high into the air.

Duncan staggered back toward the goal. He grabbed the crossbar to keep from falling.

The whistle blew. Any ball off the goalie's helmet or mask — unless it bounces into the goal — gives the possession to the defenders. The Thunder had possession.

Michael could see Duncan shake his head to clear his vision. Then he took the ball from the ref and dumped it into Vince's racket. The Thunder began walking down the floor.

One Gaels point came in hard, forechecking in desperation. But Vince dodged around him and passed to Walt, who passed it on to Jack.

The ball firmly in the pouch, Jack jogged down the court, one eye on the opposing players and one on the clock.

Vince headed for the bench, panting hard.

"Reilly!" yelled Coach Vickers, realizing that Michael was closest to the gate for a quick change.

As soon as Vince hit the exchange area, Michael sprinted onto the floor.

Fifteen seconds, fourteen seconds ...

With possession and a one-goal lead, the Thunder needed only to run out the time. They passed the ball around the outside. Michael moved in fast, yelling at Jack, who hit him with a pass as he came down the centre.

Michael sprinted directly into the attack zone and did a two-step to avoid two checks, happily running out the clock.

Just before the buzzer sounded, he zapped a shot at the Gaels goal.

It wasn't a difficult shot, and Michael watched it all the way in. But instead of scooping the ball and passing, the Gaels goalie pushed his head far to one side so the ball clunked off his face mask.

Whistle. Automatic goalie possession.

Michael looked at the clock. Nine seconds.

The Gaels called a time out.

The Thunder poured onto their bench. "You dork," Vince said, glaring at Michael.

"I thought …"

Coach Vickers held up one hand. "None of that. We've got nine seconds to hold them. Let's do it. Vince, Walt, Zak, Sean, Jack. Michael, back on the bench."

Those last nine seconds were the longest of Michael's life. His stomach crunched in knots as he watched the Gaels storm around the net, dogging, ducking, passing, looking for that one chance to beat Duncan.

Finally, with the clock running out, Powless fired a hard shot that hit Duncan in the midsection before it bounced up and over the goal. The buzzer sounded.

"Six to five," said Michael as the team left the bench.

"No thanks to you," said Vince without looking at him.

6 Part of the Team

After the game, the Thunder gathered in the courtyard in front of the Iroquois Park Arena seeking relief from the heavy August heat. In the parking lot, merchants had set up tents to sell souvenirs: shirts, sticks, necklaces, books, and trinkets. Others offered snacks of all kinds: ice cream and soda pop, popcorn and hot dogs, hamburgers and sizzling slices of stale pizza.

Michael selected a slice of pepperoni pizza and a juice.

"Well, what are we going to do now, Michael?" asked his mother. "Anybody like to have a singalong?"

"Mom," said Michael, shaking his head.

Michael knew that that his mother never travelled far without her guitar. It might be in the car or — if his luck held — back at the hotel room where just maybe it would be too far away to easily fetch.

"So they tell me that you almost got a goal, Honeybun," she went on as they walked back to join the team. "That's great! I'm sorry I missed it. That was just at the end of the game, when Rebekah scooted out of sight and I had to track her down."

"That's okay," said Michael. He didn't blame Rebekah, and actually was glad that no one in his family had seen his big mistake.

Vince turned, his mouth half full of hot dog. "Yeah, we're going to rename him Almost Reilly."

Mrs. Reilly ignored the comment. "Well, back at the hotel tonight we could all have a little singalong. What do your friends think?"

"I'd rather someone pack me in ice and stuff me in a cooler," said Duncan.

To the south, the line between the sky and the water of Lake Ontario wavered into milky grey.

"There's gonna be a storm, I think," said Coach Vickers. "Be good to get some rain to squeeze some of this humidity out of the air."

"Any word on Jordan?" asked Duncan's mother. "Is he going to be okay?"

"His dad hasn't called yet. I didn't want to bother him until after the game. They were going to do some extra tests. But I'm sure he'll let us know as soon as he can."

Rebekah tugged on her mother's skirt, asking for an ice cream bar. Then she said she wanted a can of pop.

"There's too much sugar in that," was the reply.

"You'll be bouncy, bouncy, bouncy if I give you that."

"I'm bouncy now, see? Bounce, bounce, bounce." She jumped up and down several times, her blond hair flying. "I am flying."

"Flying princesses need to calm down a bit. You're making me dizzy just watching you," laughed Coach Vickers. "Anyway, pass the word for the team. My van is over in the parking lot not far from the skateboard run. You'll see it. There's going to be fruit drinks and some snacks. Everybody should take it easy until we find out the standings after the Warriors–Green Gaels game."

"Thank you, but I think we're going to head back to the hotel room," said Mrs. Reilly. "Do you want to come, Mikey?"

Michael winced at his mother's nickname. "I'll stay with the guys," he said.

"But," said Rebekah, "we can play paper-scissors-rock like we did in the car."

"Not now," Michael replied. "I'll stay with the guys."

"That okay?" Mrs. Reilly asked the coach.

"No problem. We'll just try to help these guys avoid tiring themselves out before the next game. The standings are tight, so we don't know which final we play tomorrow. If the Warriors win, we play them. If the Gaels win, the teams are in a three-way tie, and tie-breaker rules apply. I'd like everybody at my pavilion by seven so we know what's up."

"Pavilion?" asked Vince.

"The canopy over my van. In the parking lot. If you can't make it there, we'll post something in the hotel lobby tonight. Now, you guys rest and cool off."

The sun pressed down hard and yellow. The humid air made Michael's shirt cling to his body.

"Mikey," said Vince in a mocking tone.

Michael swallowed hard at the nickname. "It's Michael," he said finally.

"What's that, Mikey? You have something to say?"

"My name's Michael."

"But no, it's not. I heard it right from your Mom-Mee. What is it? She gone back to the hotel to get your blankie?"

"It's *Michael*," Michael repeated.

"Oh, here's Mr. Grownup, the guy who almost cost us a game. You're going to get all 'Michael' on us now, are you?" Vince laughed. "That's good. We could use more backbone from you during our games."

"It's Michael. Except for my mother. Only my mother calls me Mikey. You saying you want to be my mother?"

The surrounding players laughed.

"He got you there, Vince," said Duncan.

"A good one," agreed Walt.

Vince waved it off. "Let's head over to the park and find some shade." He turned to his teammates, ignoring Michael. "Do we really have to include the dork in this?"

Some of the group had begun to mumble agreement when Duncan spoke up. "Reilly's okay. He's on my league team. Besides, he set up that one goal for you last game. What's the problem?"

The mumbling stopped, and the group looked at Vince for his reaction. Vince glowered back, first at Duncan, then at the others, and finally at Michael.

"Whatever," he said. "I don't care if he plays tagalong."

Michael stayed beside Duncan as they all walked across the parking lot to the traffic lights at the corner. From there they could see Lake Ontario and the masts of several sailboats at the Whitby Yacht Club.

"Hey, there's a pond!" said Walt. "Maybe we could go swimming."

"That's no pond," said Michael. He had looked up Whitby on a map weeks before the tournament. "It's Lake Ontario. If you sailed straight south, you would end up in the United States."

"Mr. Geography," said Brandon.

"And Camp X was not far from here," Michael added. "I read about that. It was a camp where they trained spies during the Second World War. They had all sorts of adventures."

Michael's dad had told him that the writer of *Charlie and the Chocolate Factory* had trained there as a spy.

And so did Ian Fleming, the man who wrote the James Bond stories. Michael had watched both the *Charlie* movies, but had only heard his parents talk about James Bond, the spy known as Double-O Seven. His father had insisted that some of the amazing stuff in the Bond movies came from Camp X.

"Want to go there?" asked Duncan.

"Do they still train spies there?" asked Vince. "That'd be neat."

"Is it far?" Brandon asked.

Michael smiled. "Six, maybe seven kilometres. I checked it out on an Internet map. It's right on the lake, between Whitby and Oshawa."

"Six kilometres!" said Duncan. "That's a marathon!"

"About sixty times up and down the arena," said Michael.

"Yeah, we likely run that far in a game," said Zak. "At least, those who have regular shifts, Michael."

Everybody laughed.

"Not Duncan!" said Vince. "He gets out of breath getting to the edge of his crease."

"Do not," said Duncan. "Besides, I get just as sweaty as anybody out there. You should try playing in the heat wearing a ton of padding. It's too bad there isn't a breeze today," he added. "Then we could have tied a string to Walt and used him as a kite!"

They crossed the road and headed for a field that

was bare except for soccer nets. In the distance they could see a group playing soccer. "Hey, want to play a game?" Duncan asked.

"We have no soccer ball, nerd," Brandon said.

"We could join those guys," Walt said, pointing across the park almost two soccer fields away.

"Nah, it's too hot."

"What do you want to do?" asked Walt.

"I don't know. What do you want to do?" replied Duncan.

After a short silence, it became obvious that they had run out of ideas. Vince said, "My dad said there is a hospital right across the street from the arenas. Why don't we go there and see how Jordan is doing?"

They crossed the street to a park. Masts from sail-boards along the lake stuck up like matchsticks. Zak pointed out a partly rusted sign. It was a big blue cross.

"What's it say?" said Vince, who didn't like to read.

"Lakeridge Health, Whitby, blah, blah, blah," said Duncan, who loved to read anything. He and Michael often traded books.

"Let's go there and see if Jordan is going to be ready to play tomorrow," said Vince.

"Do you think he's in that hospital?" asked Duncan.

Vince looked smug. "I don't think you have to be a brain surgeon," he said. He turned and pointed to the Iroquois Park complex across the street. "That's where he got hurt." He turned and pointed to a large stone building that looked like it belonged on a movie set for the Flintstones. "The hospital."

He did it again. "Rink. Hospital. Rink. Hospital. Do you think they'd take him back home to Bowmanville to the hospital there?"

Duncan shrugged. "I don't know. I guess they'd take him here."

"So, do we want to go, or what?" Vince started to lead the way without waiting for an answer.

Since they were all following Vince toward the hospital, the decision seemed to have been made.

They headed across the park in a direct line to the hospital. At the edge of the soccer field, Vince stopped and picked up some stones. A flock of Canada geese waddled by, honking once or twice before lifting briefly to the air and settling a few metres in front of them.

Vince whipped a stone at the birds. They flew off again.

"Hey!" said Duncan, turning. "Leave the geese alone. They didn't hurt anybody. They got as much right to be here as you do."

Vince kicked at the grass. "Do I have as much right to poop on the grass?" he asked. "Besides, I'll throw if I want to."

As they neared the hospital, they could see who the soccer players were. "Hey, it's the Warriors!"

said Walt.

"They're the guys who put Jordan in the hospital," said Vince.

"I sure hope we play them tomorrow," said Duncan. "I want to shut them out."

"Good luck with that," said Vince.

One of the geese landed near the edge of the field by the soccer players. Vince lined up and threw his last stone at it, hard, with a side-arm pitch.

"Hey! Don't do that!" said Duncan.

Michael's eyes followed the flight of the stone. *It must be flat*, he thought remembering the time he had looked up the physics of skipping stones. He saw it curve up and over the geese before making a wide curve to the left and sailing through the air toward the soccer players.

When it became obvious that the stone was not going to miss the scrum of players, Michael shouted a warning: "Heads up!"

The soccer players stopped dead and stared at the Thunder players.

"Ouch!" one yelled, and then crouched down on one knee, his hand up to his head behind his ear. "That hurt!"

"The bugger threw a stone!" one of the Warriors shouted.

"He hit Ryan!" a voice rang out.

One of the Warriors picked up a stone — likely

the one that had been thrown, Michael thought, since the park was grass-covered — and sent it winging back at the Thunder players.

But it was just one stone and, unlike the stone out of the blue at the Warriors, the Thunder players were all watching for it, so it was easy to step aside. It missed hitting anyone.

"Ryan's bleeding!" said one of the Warriors.

Ryan straightened up, still rubbing his head. He charged toward the Thunder players. "Let's get them!"

Suddenly the whole group of Warriors was racing at Michael and his teammates. The only player Michael recognized was Abrams, his nemesis from the game earlier that day. He was tall and lean, with light brown skin and dark brown eyes, his hair cropped short. Michael looked around for refuge, but could see only the sailboats bobbing at the far side of the park and the hospital three or four arena lengths down the road.

"Their guys hit Jordan!" yelled Vince.

"Let's get them back!" said Brandon. They turned as a group to jog toward the Warriors.

The two groups merged into a confusion of boys. There was pushing and shoving. Someone elbowed Michael in his aching rib. He pulled away and moved to the edge of the group.

Michael saw Duncan, standing with his feet solidly planted, swinging his fists, hitting no one but daring anyone to come closer. A few steps away, Vince held a guy by the shoulders. They looked as though they were locked forehead to forehead, like two fighting mountain goats.

Michael now found himself edging away. Even further away he saw Abrams, who now moved a step towards him.

"What's the matter?" Abrams said. "Trying to run away?"

Michael glared at him. "Run? No, I was just trying to make sure that you didn't."

"Chick-chick-chick-chicken," Abrams taunted. But he made no move. Michael eyed him warily, circling to his right.

"Sure," Michael said, "pick on the smallest kid in the group." He wasn't sure, but he thought he saw a flick of a smile. Abrams moved sideways.

Before Michael could decide what to do, a shrill blast of a whistle pierced the air. Two men waded into the mix-up, holding pairs of squirming boys apart, pushing others away. One lifted Vince and a Warrior off their feet with opposite hands, leaving the two flailing aimlessly and kicking at air that provided no traction.

"Okay, kids, break it up, break it up."

The two men stood solidly, each holding two boys by the arms and keeping the two groups apart with scowls. One of them had a whistle hanging around his neck.

"What's this all about?" he asked. "I've never seen anything like this, even in a game. What's going on here?"

It was the referee from their game with the Warriors.

7 Caught

The referee held Vince and the Warrior each firmly by the upper arm.

"So what is it all about?" he asked. "Lacrosse players in a fight? I am surprised."

No one spoke.

"And you two," the ref said to Michael and Abrams, standing slightly apart from the group. "What's your part in all this?"

Michael wanted to say that he was not fighting, but one glance from Vince made him reconsider. The Warrior next to Vince tried to slip from the grasp of the ref.

"Don't be impatient, now," said the ref. "I think we have to get straight who we have here." Both men released their grips on their charges at the same time, as though they had agreed by a hidden signal.

"I recognize you guys. I refereed your game yesterday. My name is Wade Diamond. This man is Scotty

Martin. Now can someone tell me what's going on?" Michael swallowed hard. Scotty Martin. National coach. Hall of fame.

"So?" Ref Diamond prompted.

Duncan swallowed hard and then piped up. "Well, these guys ..." Then he faltered.

"These guys what?" asked Scotty Martin. "Do you want to tell me what these guys did?"

"*These* guys were throwing rocks," said one of the Warriors. When he saw anger start to cross Ref Diamond's face, he added, "At the geese. They were throwing rocks at the geese."

Ref Diamond and Scotty Martin looked at all the boys, from one face to another, searching. Michael looked at the ground.

"I take it you didn't like that," said Ref Diamond to the Warrior. After a silence, he added, "That wasn't a question."

He tapped Michael on the shoulder.

"Look up here, son. Way up. Is that what happened?" Michael wondered if he was being centred out because of his size. Did they expect he'd talk from fright? He knew he could easily use his words to defend the team.

Michael looked at Abrams, then Vince, before answering. "That's right, Mr. Wade, sir. We were throwing rocks. At the geese."

"It's Ref Diamond."

"Sorry, sir."

Out on the soccer field, a dozen or more Canada geese rose honking into the air. Michael could hear the flapping of their wings. A sailboat made its silent way along the waterway.

"Shut up, Reilly," said Vince, in a harsh whisper that everyone could hear.

Then Ref Diamond turned to Vince. "No, I think we should hear more of what our friend here has to say. What is your name, son?"

"Michael Reilly, sir."

"Tell me more about this rock throwing. Help me to understand."

Michael blinked, and was afraid that tears would come. He felt a lump in his throat.

"We didn't mean anything by it," he said slowly. "The geese were just, er, there. So we thought we'd scare them off. We were just heading over to the hospital to see how our friend is doing."

"You have a friend in the hospital?" asked Scotty Martin.

"Yes, sir, Mr. Martin. He fainted after the game yesterday, and his father took him to the hospital. He wasn't back for our game today."

"I see."

Ref Diamond nodded. "I heard about that."

"And his father got kicked out," said Vince.

"Oh, I see," said Ref Diamond, making the

connection for the first time.

"And then what?" asked Scotty Martin.

"Well, we were going across the field here and I guess we kind of started scaring the geese just to see what would happen," said Michael.

"And what did happen?"

"Well, for one thing, they flew in the air," said Michael. "But then … then we decided to wrestle with these other guys."

The two men exchanged glances.

"Wrestle. So it was kind of a play fight? Not real." Scotty Martin looked dubious. "So these guys," he said, gesturing toward the Warriors, "were in a wrestling match to defend the geese?"

Somebody snickered.

The heat of the late afternoon pressed down. In the silence, Michael could hear a swish of breeze and the gentle roar of the expressway. He could smell the goose poop on the grass near the water's edge.

Michael couldn't trust his voice from breaking into tears from the stress, and his teammates were looking at anyone but him. "Yeah," said one of the Warriors, finally. "That's the way it was."

"Yes," said Vince.

"Yes," repeated other members of the Thunder.

"Yeah," agreed the Warriors.

Scotty Martin straightened up to his full height. Michael thought the man was probably about his father's age. He was lean. His arms looked rock solid, and his dark eyes glinted.

"So you guys play on what team? The Thunder, from Clarington?"

Vince nodded.

Turning to the other team, he said, "And you guys are Warriors." He stated. "Right, Mr. Abrams?"

Abrams nodded.

"I'd like to believe your story," Ref Diamond broke in. "But I'm going to have to report this. We have one player now in the hospital with an injury in this tournament. I'm not going to take a chance that there will be others. Sorry."

"What's that mean?" asked Vince. "Who are you going to report it to?"

"The tournament officials have to be informed," he said. "And that means that both your teams may be suspended from the tournament."

"Suspended?" said Abrams. "That's not fair."

"We didn't do anything!" Vince protested.

"It's up to the tournament officials to decide what's fair here," said Scotty Martin. He and Ref Diamond stood, the ref with his arms crossed, while the two groups separated.

The Warriors slowly returned to the soccer field, while the Thunder continued across the street to the hospital. At the entrance they learned from construction workers that the hospital was closed for repairs.

Jordan would have been taken to the hospital in Oshawa ten or more kilometres away — too far to walk, even without a simmering heat wave with humidity that made sweating no fun.

They headed back to the arena, and walked for a while in silence. Finally Vince spoke.

"What do you mean, geese?" he asked Michael. "And a wrestling match? The last I looked you were heading north on a fast horse. Even the Warriors think you're chicken."

"I'm not," Michael replied.

"Well, this time your mouth maybe got us all in trouble. You know that, don't you, Einstein? That's why you don't play regular shifts. You're afraid of taking a hit. You just did it again."

8 One for All

Back at the arena, Michael checked the bulletin board for information on the final pairings.

"What does it say?" asked Vince.

"Nothing yet," Michael told him. "The chart is still blank."

"If the ref reports us, we're done," Vince said. "If we get kicked out and the Warriors don't, that would be *really* unfair."

Michael wondered how Vince could blame the Warriors and not mention his part in throwing the rock. He said nothing.

But Duncan spoke up. "Anyone who throws rocks shouldn't live in glass houses."

"How was I to know?" said Vince. "It's not as though I meant to hit a goose or anything."

"But you did hit a Warrior, even if it was just a nick," said Duncan. "There is that."

Michael said, "I read about this baseball player with

the Yankees who beaned a seagull in Toronto one time."

"You're kidding," scoffed Duncan.

"Killed him. The seagull, I mean. The next day the police charged him."

"They wouldn't do that, would they?" Duncan looked worried. "For killing a seagull?"

"They did," said Michael. "But the judge let him off. The player's name was Dave Winfield. Google it. It was years and years ago."

On the walk back to the hotel room, Vince broke the silence. "About that guy and the seagull," he said. "He got off, right?"

Michael nodded. "Eventually," he said.

Vince hesitated for a moment to let that sink in. "So I think that we should stonewall," he said. "Nobody saw me throw the stone. Aside from you guys. Make them prove it."

Brandon said, "This isn't just about you, Vince. And it's not all about throwing rocks at geese."

They stopped at a traffic light, waiting for the walk signal. "We've told Ref Diamond and Scotty Martin what happened," said Michael. "That's pretty well what happened. Anyway, that's now the team story and we should stick to it."

"That's right," said Duncan. "We're all in this together."

In the hotel lobby, Coach Vickers had taken a big

sheet of newsprint and drawn a pairings chart. The scores of the previous day's games had been inserted. Someone had left greasy fingerprints on the paper.

"Well, we're not kicked out yet," said Vince. "At least, according to that."

"So it comes down to today's game between the Warriors and the Gaels," Michael said. "We'll meet the winner in a playoff for the Group A championship."

"If we're still in the tournament," added Duncan.

"When do the Warriors and Gaels play?"

"According to this, they're playing at seven o'clock." The clock on the wall behind the lobby desk said five-thirty.

Michael liked to follow the flow of the charts, and add up points. He liked it best when some tournaments scored points for each period. The more numbers the better.

"So what happens if we all end up tied?" asked Walt. "Is there a tie-breaker?"

"They'll likely go to goals-against," said Vince. "Maybe total periods. Something like that."

Walt looked puzzled. "How does that work?"

"Well, a team that wins a game gets two points," explained Michael. "If it's a tie, each team gets one point."

"Duh."

"But then if they count each period, a team gets one point for each period they win."

Vince pondered for a moment. "You mean a team could lose and still get more points than the team that won?"

"How do you mean?" Michael couldn't believe that Vince was asking him a straight question.

"Well, if a team won three periods, they'd get three points, but the team that won the game would get only two."

Michael tried to explain without a paper and pencil to write things on. "But if a team won three periods they'd win the game and have five points. A team could win two periods by scoring one goal each in the first two periods and be up two to nothing, and then let in three goals in the third to lose three to two. They'd score two points, and the winning team would score three points: one for the period they won and two points for winning the game."

"Oh," Vince didn't look completely convinced, but obviously didn't want more numbers thrown at him.

"So when will we know?" Duncan asked.

Michael looked at the clock. "We'll know this evening."

Mrs. Reilly and Rebekah came into the lobby carrying a bucket of fried chicken.

"Dinner, Michael," said his mom, holding up the bag. She looked at Duncan, Vince, and Walt. "You want to join us? There's enough."

"Sure," said Duncan, who had often stayed at the Reillys' for meals.

"Me, too," said Walt.

Vince looked uncomfortable and shrugged. "I'll pass," he said.

Back in the Reillys' room, they snapped open cans of soda pop, and munched on chicken bones held in tiny tattered paper napkins with greasy fingers. They had just finished when a knock sounded on the door. Coach Vickers came in, red in the face and obviously angry.

"We've got trouble," he said. "I want everyone in the dining hall in fifteen minutes."

Vince caught up with Michael in the corridor. "What's this about?" Vince whispered as they filed into the hall. "Do you think we've been suspended already?"

Michael shrugged. It wasn't seven o'clock yet. The Warriors–Gaels game would not have started.

When the players had edged into the room, squeezed into corners, and been swept off tables by shushing parents, the coach held up one hand and everyone went silent.

Coach Vickers kept that hand in the air for a moment while he checked to see that everyone on his team was in attendance.

"We have a problem," he said at last.

The tone of his voice killed every joke waiting to

be cracked.

"Several members of our team have been in a fight," the coach explained quickly. "Somebody started throwing rocks. One of the kids on the Warriors team was hit on the head and seriously hurt. The word is he is in the hospital. There's a lot of talk right now about what's going to happen. The incident has been reported to the tournament officials, and that means we are likely going to be suspended. Kicked out of the tournament. 'We' means the Thunder, this whole team."

Silence. "No team of mine has ever had this happen before. I want to know what's going on."

Many heads hung low. Finally, Vince spoke up. "It didn't happen like that."

"Vince. I'm disappointed."

"But it wasn't …"

"There is a kid who got hit in the head with a stone. So whatever you were trying to say it wasn't — it was!"

Michael tried to follow the sense in that sentence and gave up.

"I think we'd better start at the beginning," said the coach. "Who was involved? And can someone fill me in on what exactly did go on? Brandon, what about you?"

Brandon examined his shoelaces.

Michael raised his hand.

"We were just going to the hospital to try to find out about Jordan," he said. "And we met the other guys by accident."

"The other guys?"

"The Warriors."

"Did you start throwing rocks by accident?" asked Coach Vickers.

Michael looked up to see his mother staring at him. "Well? I'm waiting."

Michael repeated, "We were just going to check on Jordan."

"You said that once. That may be a good story, but it's not true. That's not the hospital they took Jordan to."

"I know," said Michael. "We found that out afterwards."

"After what? Go on, Michael."

"We were walking through the park. The one with the soccer fields. And some Warriors were playing soccer. We started to throw stones at the geese. To make them move. Then ..." He looked over at Vince. Vince threw Michael dark looks through angry eyes.

"Then some of the Warriors were playing soccer," Michael pushed on. "And one of the stones was like a wild pitch, and nicked one of the Warriors. So then they came up to us, and told us to leave the geese alone. And then we said, 'Or what?' and then somebody started shoving. That's about it."

"That's it?"

Michael nodded. He tried to remember what he had told Ref Diamond that afternoon.

"So who was involved? Brandon? Michael? Who else? Walt?"

From the corner, Duncan slowly got to his feet. "And me," he said. "I was there, too."

The coach looked deflated, as though he was an air mattress someone had stuck with a pin. He breathed out and made a swooshing sound.

"Do any of you want to add anything more?" he said finally.

The whole team, parents and all, sat stunned.

Finally, Vince stared at the floor and raised one hand weakly. "Me, too," he said. "I was there."

Coach Vickers let out a slow breath in exasperation. "What disappoints me most are two things. First, that you didn't come to tell me right away. And second, that you are lying about it. I heard all about the rock throwing, and how that kid got hit on the head. I hope you all realize what this does to the sport of lacrosse. This is the type of thing that ends up on the front page of newspapers or on the national news on TV — kids involved in sports and fighting. It doesn't take a genius to see how the media could turn this into a racial incident."

He paused. Michael had not thought of that. He exchanged looks of surprise with Duncan and Vince.

A racial incident? Why, he thought, do adults make everything complicated?

"It happened in hockey a couple of years ago and somebody took a video. Guess what everybody saw? Not the hours of practice the team put in, not the team-building that goes into a great team, and not the satisfaction. No, what people saw was a bunch of kids trying to punch each other out. That's not sports — that's hooliganism."

"Don't be too hard on them," said one of the parents. "The pros do it ..."

"The pros are conditioned and trained and get paid a lot of money. But even that doesn't make it right. I don't want my team playing gangland rules. I'd rather have them not play. And the pros don't do it in the parking lots. No matter what the rules are in the game, in the real world fighting is criminal."

Michael finally raised his hand again.

"You have more, Michael?"

"Yes, sir." Michael swallowed hard. "Some of that information isn't exactly true."

"You're going to enlighten me?"

"Sir, nobody got hurt like that. One of the Warriors got nicked by a stone, but it was just a scratch."

Coach Vickers crossed his arms. "So you say. I heard otherwise from a good authority."

This time it was Michael who felt deflated.

"Okay, guys," Coach Vickers said when he saw that

nobody else had anything to say, at least not in public. "The team can go now. I want to meet with the parents for a few minutes. We haven't heard officially, but this tournament may be over for us."

The team filed slowly out of the room. To no one in particular, Duncan asked, "What is goolihanism?"

9 The Team Story

When she got back to the hotel room, Michael's mother picked up what was left of their fried chicken dinner: paper plates of greasy fries, gnawed bones, and half-eaten blobs of coleslaw. Rebekah fussed with her princess dolls on a small round table by the window.

"That isn't really eating healthy," Michael said, trying to smile. But his mother remained grim-faced, her mouth stretched in a firm, straight line.

"Well," she said finally. "What have you got to say for yourself?"

"Nobody meant to —"

"But you did. You and your teammates ended up fighting with another team. That's not why we drive you all over the country to play lacrosse. That's not why we pay the registration fees."

"I'm sorry," said Michael. "I want to be a good teammate to the guys, but I want to tell the truth, too. Now some of the team blames me just because I spoke up."

Rebekah knelt on a chair and placed a perfect little princess inside a tent she had made out of a magazine on the table near the window.

"Runzel's going camping," she said. She ran her tongue across her upper lip. "But Runzel would rather be home in her castle." She looked directly at Michael. "So if you get suspended you couldn't play any more, right?"

Michael nodded.

"Then we'd have to go home. Goodie. I hope you get suspended."

"Michael, you know what is most important, and I know you'll do what's right," Mrs. Reilly said "But right now the coach and the team manager are planning on calling it all off anyway rather than wait to be suspended."

"But they can't do that!" said Michael.

"Hear that, Runzel?" said Rebekah. "We're going home. Wheee!"

Michael turned to his sister. "Why don't you grow up? This isn't about you and your dolls."

"No, it's about you playing lacrosse. It's always about you and your boring game. Are we going home now, Mom?"

"Not quite yet, Bekah," said her mother. "We'll wait for the official word."

Michael picked up his spare lacrosse stick. "I'm going out to toss balls."

"In this heat?" his mother asked. "Why not stay here where it is cooler?"

He shrugged. "I'll just be outside," he said as he left the room.

In the parking lot at the end of the building, Jason Walt and Vince were tossing balls back and forth.

"If it ain't the guy who ratted the team out," said Jason.

"I didn't rat," said Michael. "I just —"

"Yes, you did," said Walt. "Coach didn't know anything. He was just fishing. He had heard a rumour, that's what my dad said. So you confirmed the rumour."

"And it's your fault, Reilly," added Jason. "You and your big mouth. What a loser. We don't even need you on the team to warm benches."

Michael felt his chin tremble.

"So now coach is going to pull us out of the tournament so we won't get suspended," said Vince.

Michael realized that he was being bullied, and he knew it was not fair. "Me? I wasn't the one who threw the rock!"

"Yeah, you didn't even fight," said Vince, laughing. "In fact, I think you started running in the other direction."

Duncan and Zak came around the corner.

"Hey, it's Motormouth," said Zak.

"Yeah, we're just talking about how Einstein here has got us all kicked out of the tournament," said Vince.

"Don't call me that," said Michael. "Einstein was a scientist and wrote books. Books about the theory of relativity, and the speed of light. But I guess you wouldn't know anything about that kind of speed, Vince."

"You're as funny as a kick in the crotch, Reilly," said Jason.

"And you have to be careful about that area, Jason. Too close to a head wound," Michael said, turning on his other teammate.

It took Duncan about two seconds to realize what was going on. "How come you guys are picking on Michael?" he asked.

"Because he's King Rat," said Jason.

"And because he runs away when there's a fight," said Vince.

Michael tossed the lacrosse ball once against the wall of the hotel, then held it in the webbing of his stick. He walked up to Vince, who was taller by half a head.

"I wish you'd make up your mind," he said. "Either I ran away when there was a fight or the fight was all my fault. Either I went running to the coach to get us thrown out of the tournament or I made up stuff and lied to try to get us off the hook. It can't be both."

"Well, it is both," said Vince. "Because you did start to run. I saw you. And then you tried to say that we were in a wrestling match. Then you told the coach that it was nothing but some shoving."

"Well, wasn't it? And I was not the one who threw the rock."

Vince opened his mouth to say something but seemed to have forgotten the words before he could get them out.

"The stone was an accident," said Duncan. "It would have made a good skipping stone, that one. Did you see it curve?"

"Yeah, we saw," said Walt.

"And it didn't conk that guy on the head. It nicked him. That's all."

"Michael never did anything," Duncan continued. "In fact, he's the one that got us out of trouble. Remember, back there? He's the one who told them about the geese, and the Warriors protecting the geese. You know. Like he told the coach."

"He made that up," said Jason. "Didn't he?"

"But that's part of the problem," said Duncan. "There are too many people who weren't there who think they know what happened. If I remember, you weren't there, Jason."

"But Vince said …"

"We were all upset that Jordan got hurt. And maybe some people …" Duncan shot a look at Vince. "… thought that they got away with it because the referee was First Nations, like the Warriors. All I know is that after the kid got hit with the stone, the Warriors came at us. And I wrestled with one guy a bit. Then the ref and that other guy came along."

"Scotty Martin," said Michael.

"Yeah," said Duncan.

"Well, Reilly still blabbed to the coach," said Jason. "He could have kept his mouth shut."

"Yeah, that's for sure," mumbled Zak.

Michael picked up the lacrosse ball and started tossing it against the brick back wall of the hotel.

Whump! Whump! Whump!

"What I'd like to know is where did Coach find out about all this?" said Vince. "Now, thanks to Einstein, he thinks we're lying to him."

"I just told what happened," said Michael. "Which I think you all should."

"What, and get suspended?"

"Think about it. How did the coach find out about any of this?"

Vince intercepted the ball from Michael and hurled it back at the wall.

Whump! Whump!

"The coach found out because Michael told him," he said. "Just like I said, he blabbed."

"But he had heard something first. Remember, Scotty Martin and Ref Diamond said they had to report to the tournament officials. Think about it. What would make a little pushing and shoving that important?"

"I don't know what you're talking about," Vince said, but he started to go red.

"The Warriors are a First Nations team, and Ref Diamond is too. You said it yourself. They think we were fighting because of that. So that's the story that's going around the arena all afternoon. That means that when the tournament officials hear about it, that's the story they'll have. And we will get kicked out. Or worse. What if some reporter hears that story?"

"The only good thing," said Jason, "is that the Warriors would get kicked out, too."

Michael darted in front of Vince and grabbed the ball and flung it back at the wall.

Whump! Michael grabbed his own rebound, and held it. "Hold on a minute, guys. Let's think this through."

"Hey, hey, Einstein at work," mocked Vince.

"No, really," said Michael. "We can't let that decision be about suspicions of a race riot or rumours about what happened. We're going to have to get to the league officials and let them know what really happened."

"They'll never believe you," said Jason. "They know you lied."

"And they'll believe you about something you weren't even there to see?" Michael shot back. "You seem to be more interested in blaming this all on me because I told what I saw. Think about what might happen if no one said anything. Or if we got caught trying to lie our way out of it. It would be worse."

Michael threw the ball hard against the wall.

"But nobody will believe us," said Vince.

"Of course they won't believe just us," he conceded. "That's why we have to get the Warriors to go with us. If we all tell the same story, then they'll realize it was nothing. Besides, there are two good witnesses that it never got beyond a little wrestling."

Everybody ignored the last ball thrown. It bounced once on the parking lot pavement and rattled against the chainlink fence behind them.

"Get the Warriors to stick up for us?" said Vince.

"Yeah," said Michael. "Can you think of any other plan?"

A hotel employee stuck his head out of the nearest door and yelled, "Could you stop bouncing the ball against the wall? We've had complaints."

Michael scooped up the ball into his racket.

"No problem," he called so his voice would carry. "Tell them we're sorry."

The team members stared at one another as though they had discovered the source of the Nile — and found it to be poisoned.

"Okay," said Vince. "So who's going to talk the Warriors into helping us out?"

10 Running the Show

"You don't think the Warriors would help us, do you?" said Jason. "Those guys would just love to see us gone."

Michael scooped up the ball that had begun to roll back across the parking lot. "They're in the same difficulty that we are. They don't want to be kicked out of the tournament any more than we do."

"So what do we do?"

The group gathered around Michael, who suddenly found himself, the youngest and smallest member of the team, the centre of attention.

"First, we've got to convince Coach Vickers that nothing happened," said Vince. "He didn't seem to believe it. And if he doesn't, the tournament officials sure won't."

"Yeah, Mikey messed it up," said Jason.

Duncan glared at Jason. "Who peed in your corn flakes? At least Reilly tried. I thought we were going to fix this, rather than blame it on someone."

"Well, first of all we do have to tell the truth," Michael broke in before the whole group lost focus. "To everybody."

"No way!" said Jason.

Duncan grabbed the ball in his stick and bounced it. "First we have to figure out what really did happen," he said.

The group shared blank looks.

"And then we have to level with everyone," said Michael. "The Coach. Ref Diamond."

"So," said Vince, "what exactly did happen?"

"That's a good question," said Brandon.

Jason said, "Thanks to Mr. Big Mouth here, Coach Vickers believes that there was a big fight, and everybody thinks we're racist rednecks."

"So first we have to make sure he knows that it didn't happen like that," said Duncan.

"He already knows. Michael told him," said Brandon.

"He can't just know," explained Duncan. "He has to believe that it didn't happen like that. Before he does something stupid."

"He thinks you lied," Vince said to Michael. "And you kind of did. You even lied to the two guys in the park that broke up the fight."

"I wouldn't exactly call it a fight," said Michael.

"More like a shoving match," said Duncan. "Hockey players wouldn't call that thing in the park a fight."

Michael continued. "So first we have to convince the coach. Then we have to get to the ref, Wade Diamond, and Scotty Martin, and tell them exactly what happened. And then we have to get together with the Warriors and convince everybody that this didn't mean anything."

"Good idea," said Jason, "but who's going to carry the ball? If this gets messed up even more, we might as well go home. Stay home. Be known as the team that got kicked out of the provincials."

Nobody volunteered.

"What about you, Duncan?" asked Brandon. "Coach Vickers listens to you."

"No way," said Duncan, shaking his head. "I'd get my merds wixed."

"What about Einstein," said Vince, sarcastically. "He's mouthy enough."

"Or what about you, Jason?" asked Duncan. "Are you tough enough?"

"Well, duh," said Jason.

"Einstein?" repeated Vince. "Do you think you could carry it off?"

Michael looked at Vince. "You're really asking me?"

"You got the mouth," said Vince. Michael knew he was trying to be flippant, but his face said he really meant it.

The group looked to Michael.

"Are you tough enough?" Vince asked.

Michael realized that he was now in charge of whatever had to be done.

He looked Vince in the eye. "Let's do it," he said.

Duncan had already dialed the coach's number. He handed the cell phone to Michael. The ringing tone turned to a recorded voice. "No answer," he said, handing the phone back. He headed across the parking lot to the front entrance to the hotel.

"Where's he going?" he heard Duncan say behind him.

"I don't know, but I think we're supposed to follow," said Vince.

In the hotel lobby they met Mr. Shelby and Jordan. "Have you seen the coach?" Michael asked.

"Hey! Jordan!" shouted Vince. "How are you doing? You okay now?"

"The doctors said it was an electrolyte imbalance," said Mr. Shelby. "He has to be more careful to rehydrate, drink lots of water and sports drinks. But he still has a headache."

"We need to see Coach Vickers," said Michael. "Have you seen him?"

"He was in his room a minute ago," Mr. Shelby replied. "You could try there."

Michael darted down the corridor and knocked on the door to room 13. His teammates shuffled to a halt behind him, almost bumping into one another.

No answer.

Michael knocked again.

Behind the door he could hear voices and the opening of a patio door.

Knock, knock, knock.

A closet door closed. Somewhere a TV blared out the day's news. Finally, the door swung open.

It was Mrs. Vickers, with her dark eyes and long hair in curls to her shoulders.

"Where's Coach?" asked Michael. Then he seemed to remember his manners. "Sorry, Mrs. Vickers, for bothering you, but we need to see Coach Vickers."

"He's not here, Michael," she said. "He just left."

"We have to see him. It's important." He added: "It's about the, the … thing."

"You'd better hurry. He was on his way over to talk to the officials."

"He can't do that!" blurted Michael.

"Well, that's what I told him," she said. "He tried phoning the officials, but he couldn't get through on his cell phone. So he's gone to the arena."

Michael spun around and headed for the lobby and the front door.

"Let's go!" he said. "To the arena."

"That's a mile away!" said Vince.

"Then we'll have to run," Michael said over his shoulder.

He ran across the parking lot to the sidewalk. He

raced past a service station and the entrance to fast food and coffee shops. To his left, he could hear the constant roar of Highway 401, the Macdonald–Cartier Freeway, the Highway of Heroes. Behind him he could hear the footsteps of his teammates. At Brock Street he sprinted to beat the yellow light and the warning flashers. Vince and Jason had both caught up with him. The others were stranded by the lights.

They raced across the sidewalk over the expressway. Vince reached the traffic light first, just in time to continue onto the bridge over the railway. The light changed before Michael reached it. Without hesitation he veered right into the entrance to the GO transit station.

"This way!" Michael shouted. But the others were half over the bridge going the long way around. Now there were just two of them, Michael and Jason. Michael in the lead, they ran down the incline ramp, hopped the guardrail, and raced across the bus boarding ramp.

"Where're we going?" Jason panted. "We don't want to catch a train!"

Michael didn't answer. He was headed for the platform where the outbound trains boarded.

"We don't have tickets!" shouted Jason.

Michael sprinted down the stairs, excusing himself around some slower adults, and into the tunnel under the railway tracks.

"Where — ?" asked Jason, falling farther behind.

Michael had remembered the tunnel from a trip on the GO train he had taken with his father. He raced along the damp echoing tunnel, ran up two flights of steps, and emerged in the parking lot on the south side of the station. He continued across the parking lot, and crossed Henry Street into the Iroquois Park parking lot.

He slowed to a jog. *Now where?* he wondered, *Where would Coach go?*

Michael glanced to the right to where the coach had parked earlier that day. No vehicle.

Taking off again, he ran in the main door of the complex. If Coach went anywhere, it would be to the officials' room, where the schedules were made up and the results calculated.

Wherever that was.

Still panting, Michael hurried up to the information kiosk.

"Where are the tournament officials?" he asked, standing on his toes so he could better see over the counter.

"Yeah, we need to see them," said Jason, who had caught up with Michael at the doors to the complex.

"They're in the meeting room number five," said the teenaged girl behind the counter. She spoke directly to Jason. "But I don't think players are allowed ..."

"Where is room five?" Michael asked.

"We need to go there," said Jason urgently.

The teenager snapped her gum. "Whatever. Down this corridor. Third on your left."

"Thanks," they both said back over their shoulders.

Michael turned, with Jason following. Vince and Duncan caught up with them at the main door. They turned past the food court down a hallway, which got darker the farther they went, but the air got cooler, as though the air conditioning worked better the deeper they got into the territory of the officials.

The door to room number five was closed. Michael knocked.

They stood listening quietly, before repeating the knock. But from the silence on the other side of the door, Michael knew there was no one there.

To make sure, he tried the door. The handle would not turn. It was locked tight.

"Now what do we do?" asked Jason.

They returned to the concourse, worried that they were too late.

"Let's check the board," suggested Michael. "Maybe that'll tell us something."

In the main concourse, opposite the information desk, an electronic board showed the scheduled games. Below it was a large bulletin board with handwritten team standings and matches.

The charts showed the results of that day's games — all but the Gaels–Warriors game. The matching for the next day's finals had not been filled in.

Several members of the Warriors shouldered their way through the crowd, carrying sticks and equipment bags. They made their way to the bulletin board.

"Well, if it isn't the Flinstones," said one of the Warriors.

"Without a ref to protect them," said another. Michael recognized him as Abrams.

"Head hunters," said Vince. "That's what you guys are. We know what you did when you hit Jordan."

"You guys are chicken," said the tallest of the Warriors. "Throwing stones. One of our guys was hit. You guys are going to pay."

"Hey, calm down," said Michael. "Vince, zip it."

"You guys charged Jordan from behind," accused Jason.

"Oh, yeah, maybe we ought to …"

The two groups began to merge. Someone pushed.

"Hold it, hold it," said Michael, bounced off balance as the two groups began shoving.

"Watch it, shrimp," said one, pushing Michael backward.

Jason stepped forward and pushed the guy back.

Voices rose. Abrams shouted, "Enough!"

Michael stumbled and went down on one knee. When he tried to get up, he bumped his head on the underside of the bulletin board.

The pushing and shoving continued. The bulletin

board skidded to the left.

Michael got to his feet and tried to step between Jason and one of the Warriors. He bumped into Abrams, who was attempting to hold his own teammate.

"Stop, stop," Michael said. "They're going to kick us *all* out if we don't do something. We have to talk."

"Yeah, right," said one of the Warriors. "We'll be kicking you guys out, all right. We whumped the Gaels just now, and tomorrow we'll whump you."

"If there *is* a next game. If both teams are still in the tournament."

"What do you mean?" asked Abrams, as if Michael's message was sinking in.

"The ref reported that we had a fight," Michael said. "*Both teams* are going to be kicked out."

Abrams laughed. "Fat chance of that," he said, but a hint of doubt had appeared in his eyes. "Come on, guys."

"See, we're not going to be kicked out," said Jason excitedly as the Warriors disappeared down the long hall. "The Warriors would know by now."

"Maybe," Michael said. "Maybe."

11 Man-to-Mann

The Warriors went down the hall one way, and the Thunder players moved up the other. Michael found himself alone in front of the bulletin board.

At that moment, Michael wanted to be back in the hotel room. Or better yet, back home in his own room with the Rock posters, the Maple Leafs overhead light, and the bedspread with hockey rink markings on it.

He wanted to talk this over with his father. That usually helped him to feel better when he was confused and angry.

Michael thought that maybe his teammates were right, that he was a loser. They had asked him to do one thing — to talk to the Warriors and straighten out the mess. Instead, he had made things worse. *Maybe*, he thought, *everybody is right. Maybe I should have stuck to house league.*

He shuffled along the hallway. Signs pointed to the sports café. Along the walls were trophy plaques and pictures of Whitby hockey teams. He read as he went. The Whitby Dunlops, he read, were World Champions in 1958. One of the players, Bob Attersley, eventually became the mayor of Whitby.

Michael looked at the pictures in the display case.

"The last Canadian amateur team to win the World Championship," said a man's voice from behind him. Michael hadn't heard anyone approach.

"This town has produced lacrosse champions, too," the man continued.

Michael turned. It was Scotty Martin.

"Sorry, sir," said Michael.

"Sorry? Do you have something to be sorry for?"

Michael feared he would freeze solid. A small ache began in his throat, and he found it was hard to swallow.

"About that ... this afternoon ... in the park," he said finally.

"Ah, yes. That incident. Reilly, isn't it?

"You know my name?"

"You had it on the back of your sweater through both games the Thunder has played. Of course I know it. I know many names on your team. Other teams, too."

He smiled and Michael did, too. The man's voice was calm, deep — and reassuring.

"You remind me of what I was like at your age. Small, benched a lot, getting run over by anyone bigger. And right now, they're all bigger. That'll change."

Michael nodded. Mr. Martin reached into his pocket and produced a small box. He flipped open the lid. Inside were two rings, perched upright in the padding.

"Are those yours?" asked Michael. But he knew the answer.

"Yes, they are. Do you know what they are?"

"Mann Cup rings," Michael breathed. "From when you were on the Brooklin Redmen, 1985 and 1987. When you won the Mann Cup."

"You know a lot about lacrosse history," said Mr. Martin.

"The Mann Cup is the Stanley Cup of lacrosse," Michael continued. "It says so right there." He pointed to the display in the case that he had just been reading.

"Here. Try one on." Mr. Martin lifted one ring from the box and fitted it loosely over Michael's extended thumb. "It's a little big. But if you want it enough, you'll grow into it. I did."

Michael admired the ring on his hand. In the display case glass he caught a glimpse of his reflection.

"Sick!" he said.

"How hard would you work to win a ring like these?" he asked.

Michael looked up. "I'd do anything."

"When you're part of a team, you do whatever it is the team needs to be successful," Mr. Martin said.

"Combine this with a good sense of what is right, and what needs to be done, and you'll do well every time."

Michael looked up and caught the hint of a twinkle in Mr. Martin's eyes. Michael looked again at the ring, sliding loosely on his thumb.

"You've got good speed, and you handle the ball well," Mr. Martin said. "And I bet you're even better in the dressing room. Sometimes a team just needs someone who is good with words. If that's what your team needs, you do it."

Mr. Martin cleared his throat. "About that incident …"

"Yes?" asked Michael.

"Wade insisted on reporting it. He's a stickler about that, but I can't say I blame him. That's his job."

"Does that mean we're out?"

"Nobody's made a decision. Yet. Someone needs to tell your team's side of the story."

Mr. Martin held out his huge hand and smiled.

"Now give me back my ring."

12 A Truce

Michael knew what he had to do, but he had no idea how to do it.

He checked again at the bulletin board where the scores and game matchups were posted.

The score of the Warriors–Gaels game had been posted: a 9–7 win for the Warriors. But the space for the final game on Sunday was still blank. Michael did not think that was good.

A few of the Warriors walked by, still carrying their sticks. Some were eating ice-cream bars. "Hey, it's the wimp," said one. Michael said nothing.

Last in the group was Abrams. "Don't pay any attention to them," he said. "Sometimes they get carried away."

Michael shrugged. "It may not matter. Did you notice the final game isn't posted yet?" He pointed at the bulletin board.

A look of concern crossed Abrams' face. "What do

you mean? They wouldn't really cancel the final over what happened this afternoon, would they?"

"Vince didn't mean to hit that guy," Michael said. "What was his name? Ryan?"

"You mean with the stone? Of course he didn't. It was a stupid thing to do, but it wasn't on purpose. Just like your guy …"

"Jordan."

"Yeah, when Jordan got hurt in yesterday's game. He did just stumble. Nobody set out to hurt him. Don't your guys know that?"

"Not everybody."

"What's that mean?"

"The ref — what's his name, Wade Diamond? — he thinks that we were throwing stones at you guys. Or something. And that we were in a serious fight."

"Which would have been pretty stupid. But we weren't. The ref and Scotty Martin came along just in time."

"But that's not the point," said Michael. "Mr. Diamond felt he had to report it. Worse, our coach has blown it out of proportion and is ready to take us out of the tournament. If we aren't kicked out first."

Now Abrams did smile. "Do tell," he said. "You better enlighten him."

"But that's just it. We tried. He's afraid this may be a racial incident."

"Race had nothing to do with it," Abrams said. He

appeared to be realizing that not only was Michael serious, but he might be right.

Abrams looked at Michael directly. "We've got to stop them."

"That's what I have been trying to tell you," said Michael. "Will you help me to convince the tournament officials — and our coach — that what happened wasn't what they think it was? Out there in the park?"

Abrams looked out the door where the rest of the Warriors had disappeared. "As I said, they really don't believe it amounted to much. Convincing them that we should help the Thunder may be another thing. We might not get it," he said. "We can try."

***

Michael expected the Warriors to reject the story, but instead they seemed more interested in teasing him about his size than anything else.

"Hey, it's the bencher," said one.

"I can get you a little box to stand on so you can see over the boards," said another. And then they laughed.

"Guys, guys," said Abrams. "Big Thunder, here, is afraid that his team is going to be kicked out of the tournament."

Several Warriors laughed.

"Ha! We're supposed to care?"

"Yeah, then we'd just have to show up tomorrow to be the champs."

"Which we are."

Abrams raised a hand. "There's another part of this. It's about what happened in the park. What might happen is that both teams might be kicked out."

"You mean *us*?"

Abrams nodded.

"They can't do that! Nothing happened, for crap's sake!"

"Explain it to them, Mikey," said Abrams.

Michael started by telling them that the rock throwing incident was an accident. He also apologized for a few of his teammates who thought the Warriors had hurt Jordan on purpose, and explained that Jordan's collapsing after the game just made things worse.

"But now," he said, "our coach and maybe the tournament officials think this whole thing is …"

"Racial," said Abrams. "And both our teams may be kicked out."

"You mean we wouldn't get a chance to wipe out these guys in the final?" asked one Warrior.

"They may cancel the final game," said Abrams.

"We can't let it happen," Michael concluded.

"So they actually believe it was a … a … race

riot?" asked a Warrior. "Really? I didn't think it was anything like that."

The team stood around, silent, some of them even with open mouths.

"So is this just you that wants to go to talk to the officials, or is the rest of your team behind you?" asked Abrams.

Michael pretended he had no doubts about team support. "They're behind me one hundred and ten per cent. Nobody wants to be kicked out of the tournament."

The Warriors nodded, one by one, and finally Abrams said: "Okay. What do we have to do?"

Michael had the answer to that one ready. "First," he said, "we need to find Coach Vickers. He needs convincing."

"He shouldn't be hard to find," said Abrams.

"I wish. I've been looking."

"Come on," said Abrams. "First let's find your teammates."

It didn't take long for the Warriors, led by Michael and Abrams, to find the few members of the Thunder who had been involved in the incident. They were found wandering the concourse of the complex, still looking for Coach Vickers.

Despite some strange looks from his teammates, Michael explained the situation.

"Haven't seen the coach," said Duncan.

"Try calling him again," Michael said, exchanging knowing looks with Abrams. Michael handed his phone to Duncan. After four rings, the coach's muffled voice answered, "Yeah? What is it, Duncan?"

13 Making a Case

Michael and Abrams crossed the parking lot at a brisk walk despite the heat. Behind them, members of the Warriors and the Thunder followed like a gaggle of geese.

They caught up with the coach in the parking lot as he flipped his key to unlock his van.

"I brought the guys you need to see," Michael said, turning to point to Abrams and the Warriors.

Coach turned slowly as his van said *blip-blip* and blinked its parking lights.

"Who?" the coach said, his eyes taking in the group that surrounded him.

"This is —" started Michael.

"Abrams," said the Warrior, stepping up.

"Yeah, he's, like, captain of the Warriors."

Coach Vickers nodded that he knew that.

Abrams continued. "We wanted you to know that none of us think this has anything to do with race.

Your guys did a stupid thing, and we responded stupidly, and stuff happened."

"I made some accusations about the Warriors," said Vince. "I may have got some of our team riled up a bit. And I'm the guy who threw the rock."

Coach looked dubious. "But one guy was hurt …"

Abrams motioned with his head toward one of the Warriors. "Ryan," he said. "Come here. Show the guy your head."

Ryan moved forward and stood near Coach Vickers.

"The rock curved," said Ryan. "One of your guys actually called out a warning so I was able to duck."

"Michael did that," said Vince.

"Nothing much there," said the coach, examining the wound that was only a scratch.

"We didn't ask you to look for his brains," said one of the Warriors.

"But you guys were fighting," said the coach.

Abrams said, "It was no fight. If it was a fight do you think these guys would be still standing?" He grinned, although it was clear the coach didn't enjoy the humour. "The ref and Scotty Martin came along. But it was nothing," said Abrams. "Like Scotty Martin said, we'd rather keep this whole thing about lacrosse."

"And Vince certainly won't throw stones again, even when there aren't geese around," said Michael. "I'll see to that."

Coach Vickers turned to Michael and Vince. "Okay, you've convinced *me*. But it may be too late. And you may have to tell that story over again to the tournament officials. Come with me, all of you." He turned and started back to the complex.

"Don't forget to lock your car," said Duncan. Without turning, the coach extended his arm behind him and blipped the van doors locked.

Following Coach Vickers, the group of players from both teams walked quickly into the complex main door and directly to a committee room.

"Wait here," the coach said as he entered the room.

Moments later he reappeared at the door.

"Reilly, Abrams, come in," he said. "The rest of you just wait."

Michael started to follow, and then turned back to his teammates with an open-hand shrug. Vince gestured with a pushing motion. "Go on," he said, "we're counting on you."

Michael swallowed hard and followed Coach Vickers and Abrams.

Inside, three adults sat at the opposite side of a long folding table with a top that was chipped and scarred. Each had a laptop computer. They all looked tired.

"Boys, this is the tournament director, Charley Simpson. You have to talk to her." The coach gestured toward the woman in the centre, who clicked away at a few keys on her laptop and looked up.

"So who are these guys?" she asked.

But Coach Vickers had stepped back. It was up to the players.

Michael looked first at the coach and then Abrams, and finally said, "Ma'am, we're from, I mean, I'm from the Thunder. And Abrams here is—"

"Captain of the Warriors," Abrams offered.

"Tell me why I should be interested in those facts," said the tournament director.

"It's, it's …" But Abrams stumbled over his words.

"It's about an incident that happened in the park across the road," said Michael. "Earlier today. We've been told that the ref, Mr. Diamond …"

"Wade Diamond," Coach Vickers supplied.

The tournament director nodded that she understood.

"… Mr. Diamond had reported that as an incident. We …" Michael gestured toward Abrams. "That is, the players on the Thunder and the Warriors wanted you to know that he may have thought the incident was more, ah, may have misunderstood why it happened."

Charley Simpson reached out and dragged a stack of papers closer to her. She licked one thumb and started flicking through the sheets of paper.

"Here it is," she said. She went silent while her eyes zigzagged, reading down the page.

"Hmm. Okay. So what is your point." She did not say this as a question.

The room was silent. Out in the hallway, voices chattered.

"We just wanted you to know that it wasn't very serious."

"You've said that."

"I mean, it was all a mistake. One of our guys threw a rock at some geese, and missed."

"And?"

"Hit a player on our team," Abrams said. "By accident. Ryan. But it just nicked him, barely a scratch. He's outside now if you want to…"

"But a rock was thrown."

"Not at the Warriors," said Michael. "At the geese. Or toward the geese. Vince never even hit them. He just wanted to shoo them away."

"I can't imagine why," muttered the man to the left of the tournament director under his breath.

"And there was some fighting." Again, this was not a question.

"Shoving," said Michael. "It was more like shoving. And pushing. Kind of dumb stuff."

"It really was nothing," said Abrams. "We just wanted to defend the geese. Sort of a defence of nature."

The silence of the room was broken only by the voices and the shuffling sounds from the hallway outside.

"Do you have other members of your team waiting

out there?" asked Ms Simpson.

Both boys nodded.

"This is all interesting and enlightening," she said, after a pause. "But your presentation is a little late. We've already made a decision on this."

Michael felt as though he had swallowed a rock. Abrams looked stunned. Had they failed?

Abrams stepped forward. "We also wanted you to know that some people thought this might have been a racial thing," he said. "But for the Warriors, I just want you to know that we believe that this had nothing to do with it."

Ms Simpson met Abrams' gaze.

The second woman looked up. "I've been having trouble with the wireless connection here." She frowned at the boys and Coach Vickers. "All of the game pairings and tournament notices go out by e-mail and text messages so that everyone has the same information. I was just about to send it out when you came in and made your case."

Ms Simpson held up one hand. "So, what do you think?" She turned first to the woman to her right and then the man at her left. "We're the tournament committee. Sarah?"

"We've made the decision," said the woman.

"Dan?"

The man shuffled some papers. "I think we should hold back on the decision," he said. "And I think we should hear from the other team members. Then I'd like to hear from Wade again."

"Scotty Martin was there, too," said Ms Simpson.

"Do we have time to review this whole thing again?" he asked.

"Sarah?" Ms Simpson raised her eyebrows at the woman poised at her laptop.

"I thought the decision had been made."

"But it hasn't gone out yet. And I agree with Dan. If this incident brought these two fine players from two teams *together* to see us, there are more positives here than we originally thought."

She smiled at Michael and Abrams. "Maybe you could wait in the hall while we figure out the logistics."

14 Saved

The Warriors and the Thunder waited in the hallway. Everyone expected a long, boring hearing. Instead, just fifteen minutes later Charley Simpson stepped out of the committee room.

"We have a decision," she said, closing the door behind her.

No one moved. Jaws went slack.

"The incident involved was serious," she said. "Someone was injured."

"Just a scratch," said Ryan, trying to part his hair to show the mark.

"But we were impressed with the sportsmanlike conduct both teams have shown," she said. "And we are convinced that contrary to original reports, this was not a racial incident. Tomorrow we are going to see some great, fast lacrosse between two very good teams." She stood with the backs of her hands on her hips. "There will be no suspension."

Thunder and Warriors cheered together, giving each other high fives, fist bumps, Warrior to Warrior, Warrior to Thunder, and Coach Vickers to Ms Simpson.

"Now don't disappoint us," she added when the noise had died down.

"Good work, Reilly," Coach Vickers said. "You did a good job."

"Thanks."

"You think you can apply that in the game tomorrow?"

Michael smiled brightly. "I can try," he said. "I can sure try."

Minutes later, with both teams drifting into the concourse of the complex, Mr. Shelby and Jordan approached Coach Vickers.

"Well, well," said Coach Vickers. "How's our injured player doing?" He didn't mention anything about Mr. Shelby being expelled from the arena.

"I need to talk to you," said Mr. Shelby in a deep serious voice.

"I'm here," replied the coach. "Talk."

"I'd rather it be private."

"If it's about Jordan's injury ..."

"Private, please. Not in front of all the boys." Mr. Shelby looked around and recognized the Warriors mixed in with the Thunder players. "What's going on here?"

"It's a long story," said the coach. He cocked his head to one side and began walking toward the corridor to the dining room. Mr. Shelby followed, leaving the players, including Jordan, in the concourse by the bulletin board.

"Is this the guy who got hurt yesterday?" asked Abrams.

"This is Jordan," said Michael. "And yeah, he's the guy." To Jordan he said, "You okay, man?"

"I'm fine, but my dad still wants to file a complaint about my being hurt," Jordan said. "He's convinced that it was a dirty hit. But I've told him I don't remember it."

"Our coach said he saw you trip," said Abrams. "That was a bad stumble."

"Dad doesn't believe that."

The players shuffled their feet to cover the awkwardness. To fill the pause, Vince said, "Those were pretty harsh taunts your dad gave the ref."

"The ones that got him tossed out? Yeah." Jordan couldn't meet the eyes of his teammates. To Abrams and the Warriors still lingering, he said: "And he says some dumb things. He really does. He's never played lacrosse. He thinks that because a defender has two hands on the stick and pushes, it should be cross-checking."

"We almost got kicked out of the tournament," said Jason. "But Michael and Abrams here talked them out of it."

"We? Like, the Thunder?"

"We, like, Warriors and Thunder," said Abrams. "But tomorrow we're going to really send you guys packing."

"Yeah, right," said Jason.

"Well, I might not be here," said Jordan. "If coach won't agree to filing a complaint, my dad wants me to go home."

"You're kidding!" said Vince. "No way. We need you tomorrow."

"Dad said he'll likely file a complaint anyway," he said. "But if coach doesn't support it, he said that's it for me for the rest of the tournament."

Before any of the Thunder could figure out what to say, Coach Vickers and Mr. Shelby came back down the corridor. They walked a couple of metres apart. They didn't look at each other.

"Come on, Jordan," Mr. Shelby said. "We're going home."

Jordan crossed his arms and didn't move. "My team has one more game to play," he said. "I want to stay."

"Come on, son. We talked about this. There are some issues you have to make a stand on," said Mr. Shelby. "Don't let this tribe of … don't let these guys buffalo you."

But Jordan still did not budge. "Dad, you are embarrassing me."

"Embarrassing you? We talked about this, and how important it is to clamp down on violent hits. By taking a stand now, maybe you'll prevent someone else from getting hurt. It's important."

"It's lacrosse, Dad," said Jordan. "People sometimes get hurt. And I don't like your racist comments."

Mr. Shelby took a step backward. "What? Racist? You're not serious."

"Yes," said Jordan. "It's not right."

"Look, if I thought for one minute that I …you don't think … do you?"

Jordan looked his father in the eye. "Firewater," he said. "Scalp. Savages."

"And Warriors. And Braves. And Chiefs. Blackhawks. Those are sports terms," said Mr. Shelby. "I didn't …"

Abrams turned to his teammates. "Let's go, guys. We've got a game to win tomorrow."

To Michael and the rest of the Thunder he said, "We'll see you guys in the box tomorrow. And you'd better bring your running shoes."

Mr. Shelby watched the Warriors leave, then turned to Jordan. "I didn't mean anything by those comments," he said. "You don't really think I'm racist, do you? It's just a game. And I don't want you to get hurt."

"I want to play tomorrow," Jordan said.

Mr. Shelby exhaled. "I don't think you should. I

think …" He seemed to be searching for words, and failed. "It's, it's, it's — ahem … Oh, do what you want. But if you get your head cracked in, don't come running to me." Then he said, "Okay, I'll go and tell Coach Vickers."

***

When Michael got back to the hotel room later in the evening, he was almost surprised that everything looked so normal. Rebekah sat watching TV. Their mother was in the shower.

"I'm sorry if I sounded bratty this afternoon," said Michael's little sister.

"I'm not sure I follow," Michael replied.

"About being happy to go home. About wishing your team had been kicked out of the tournament."

"That's okay," said Michael. He had not realized that attending his lacrosse games was so boring for his sister. She didn't like the game; had never paid attention to it. For three years she had been playing with her dolls in the stands.

"Anyway, I'm going to give away my dolls," she said.

"What?"

"Yeah, they're for little kids."

"That'd be …" Michael was not sure what it would

be. Different, that's for sure.

When Rebekah smiled, her grin showed a gap in the front row.

"I'll even let you play with my pony dolls if you want," she said happily. "Oh, and by the way. You missed Dad when he called."

"What'd he say?"

"Nothing. Just that it's a surprise. You'll see."

"A surprise? What do you mean? Tell me."

Rebekah changed channels on the TV. "Can't," she said. "Mom wouldn't tell me what the surprise is. She said I'd just tell you."

She settled in to watch a new cartoon show. "I likely would, too."

15 Warriors vs. Thunder

Michael began the warm-up with his team on the floor of the main arena at Iroquois Park.

The arena had seating for 1,500 people and standing room for another 500. Perhaps a hundred or so people, mainly family and friends of the players, were sprinkled in the seats. Still, it easily qualified as the largest crowd his team had seen.

High in the stands his mother waved wildly. Beside her, Rebekah also gave a small wave and a smile. For the first time, she was sitting up, ready to watch the game. Michael nodded to acknowledge them.

Then he looked up again to see a figure walking down the steps toward Rebekah and his mother. His father!

Michael waved his stick. His father waved back and continued down the steps to the boards at the edge of the rink.

"I didn't think you'd make it," Michael said.

"Nor did I," said his father, his face covered with days and days of whiskers. "But I couldn't miss the championships."

"You finish the book?" His father shrugged. "Almost. Tomorrow's a holiday, so I have time to wrap up the wrinkles."

Michael was smiling so widely he thought his face would crack. "I'm glad you came."

"Me, too, son." They bumped fists, the way they often did in backyard games. "Now get out there and show us what you can do."

***

During the warm-up, Michael missed a pass from Jordan; the ball bounced three times up the floor and into the Warriors end. Michael chased it, jogging through the maze of players on the other team. Before he could reach it, Abrams had scooped up the ball from his own end zone. The Warrior looked up and saw Michael.

"This yours?" he asked with a sneer

Michael nodded.

Abrams cocked his throwing arm and tossed the ball to the Thunder end of the rink. "Keep track of your play things," he said. It was obvious that things weren't going to get easy just because they got along better outside the game.

Then the ref blew his whistle and the game was started.

Having Jordan back in the lineup made one big change: Michael was back to watching the first two shifts from the bench.

Right from the start, Michael could see that both teams were pushing the pace of the game. The play was much more end-to-end than usual, with both teams attempting to forecheck so the opponents had more difficulty organizing an attack. Michael thought it was a strategy that would benefit a team with more speed.

"Settle down, guys," Coach Vickers said every time a shift returned to the bench. "Settle down. We've got two periods to play after this one."

But Michael could see the dangers of the edgy style of play. Usually, a defending team would curl into a defensive shell around their goal, waiting for an opportunity to gain possession. Both teams seemed to be playing for fast breaks in an open game. In the second shift, the Warriors scored when they sent a man straight up through centre on a breakaway.

Fifteen seconds later, the Thunder pulled exactly the same move. Jordan hit Vince with a long pass that put him in alone. Vince went straight in, pivoted between two defenders, and fired a hard shot that bounced off the goalie's shin — and straight back out.

One Warrior scooped up the loose ball and fired a long pass up the centre. Abrams caught it over his head, and again got the ball past Duncan on a break-away.

2–0.

"We're going to get burned if they keep that up," said the coach.

Finally, Michael went on as left crease, with Vince as point and Jordan as right crease. With Thunder in possession, Duncan fielded the ball to the right corner. Vince had headed straight down the centre. The right corner flung a long pass to him, deep in Warriors territory.

But the pass was too deep and Vince couldn't reach it. The Warriors point had anticipated the long pass and intercepted it, cleanly snagging the ball out of the air, and headed hard up the centre. This left both Thunder corners scrambling to head him off. The Warrior deked around Brandon and headed in alone on goal.

Plunk!

Duncan took the shot on his helmet, whistling the play down and giving possession back to Thunder.

A glance at the bench showed the coach making dampening motions with both hands pressed flat down. *Settle down, settle down, settle down*, he was signalling.

Duncan fed the ball to Sean, who in turn got it to Vince. This time Vince had read the coach's signals and began walking the ball down the court.

Michael raced down the left side. At the faceoff

circle he tried to cut in toward the Warriors goal. Abrams blocked his way, shoving firmly with two hands on his stick, keeping him at bay.

Vince worked his way in, pivoting from his check and using his speed to avoid him. But the wall of Warriors defending their goal would not let him in. Quickly he passed to Jordan, who headed behind the goal, looking for a target. Jordan threw a pass at Michael, who grabbed it, spun once, and fired a shot on goal.

The Warriors grabbed the loose ball and headed up the floor, trying a fast break to keep the Thunder defenders off-balance.

Michael sped up the floor to keep up with the play. He could worry about catching his own check when the play reached his zone.

The Warriors didn't wait for their own team to press the advantage, or for the Thunder to create a defensive box. Instead, their point forced the defending Thunder back and fired a quick low shot at Duncan, who stopped it easily.

Duncan didn't hesitate. He sent a high soaring pass up the centre. Michael's eyes followed it as he turned and watched Vince, lagging behind the play, catch the ball in Warriors' zone, spin on his little toe, and head for the goal.

Vince had one man to beat — two, counting the goalie. He pivoted off his left foot looking for someone to take a pass. But he hesitated too long. One of the Warriors defenders caught him with a brisk cross-check. When Vince lurched back, trying to cradle the ball in his stick, the second Warriors defender whacked his stick and sent the ball flying.

In the return play, the Warriors used the fast break to create another breakaway and scored again.

3–0.

The score stayed that way until Michael's next shift. This time he was on with Dylan, Shea, and Walt. Dylan and Walt usually played crease positions with Jordan. This time Michael was to play point.

"I'm not used to that," Michael told the coach as he prepared to enter the box.

"Trust me," the coach said, and Michael was off the bench and on the floor.

Michael knew that the point is the playmaker — the central figure on attack, who can feed the ball to the shooters on the outside, or to the crease players in deep. The point must also be a scorer, able to crash the defence and shoot hard down the centre. Could he do it?

Michael went on as Duncan was taking possession in the crease and lobbing a pass to Jack on left corner. Jack jogged up the court, avoiding two checks in the process, trying to make sure that the rest of the line change had been completed. Then he passed off to Walt and headed for the bench.

Walt took the ball deep into the attack zone to the right of the Warriors goal, and passed off behind the goal to Dylan. Dylan spotted Michael coming in hard down the centre and threw a pass, which Michael reached high and nailed. Almost in one motion he came down fast and shot high and hard from four metres out.

The ball made a puny *ping* as it grazed the crossbar, then a *thud* as it bounced off the glass behind the goal. It bounced high out toward centre, repeated a series of lower bounces back down the floor, outraced all players attempting to track it down, and finally reached Duncan in the goal. Duncan scooped the ball like he was netting fish and prepared for a long throw down the box.

Clock warning. Change of possession.

Thunder players on the floor protested. Kevin argued that Michael's shot had hit the crossbar, and the shot clock should have been stopped. The ref disagreed.

On the bench, Coach Vickers turned a pale shade of purple, but said nothing.

The turnover gave the Warriors possession. Abrams took the ball and strolled easily into the Thunder defending zone. He broke quickly once around Michael, who tried to stay with him and failed. The tall Warrior crashed hard into the two Thunder corners, faked one shot, and made another, scoring over Duncan's shoulder from point-blank range.

4–0.

"Sorry, coach," Michael said when he got back to the bench.

"That one's tough to hold," the coach said. "Don't sweat it. Next time."

But next time was six shifts later when Walt came limping off with a bruised knee.

Coach slapped Michael on the shoulder. "Right crease," he said. "Play tough."

This time Michael was matched against Ryan, the Warrior who had been grazed by the stone Vince threw. He was bigger than Michael, but not much.

As he came on the floor, Michael scooped a loose ball and immediately broke fast for the Warrior zone. He glanced around. The line change had not been completed. No one was with him.

Four Warriors stood between Michael and the goal. He worked in toward the middle of the floor between the two faceoff circles, faded again to his right, and cut to the outside. He darted into the corner, hoping to draw someone to him.

He stood in the corner for a moment. The Warriors seemed to be satisfied with watching him run out the clock. Thirty seconds isn't long. He glanced up. Fifteen seconds. Fourteen. Thirteen.

Finally he took a run straight for the goal. Ryan came out to meet him. Michael pressed forward, spun, and almost from behind the net flicked a pass to Dylan coming in from his wrong side.

Dylan tried to shoot, but two defenders blocked him, knocking him off balance. Dylan struggled to keep the ball. His legs were still rubbery when the buzzer shot clock ran out.

Change of possession.

Michael ran back down the floor, easily catching Ryan and holding to him, using his stick to keep the Warrior off-balance and unable to take a pass. Ryan twisted, turned, and spun, but Michael kept with him. But Abrams was carrying the ball, and he didn't need someone to pass to. He broke in on the defensive wall, deked both corners, and sent a knee-high shot at the open net when he caught Duncan going the wrong way — only to see Duncan throw leap horizontally into the crease, knocking the ball into the corner.

The score stayed 4-0 for the Warriors.

***

At the break between the second and third periods, Coach Vickers called the Thunder to the bench.

"Good hydration," he said. "Drink as much water as you can. It's hot here today, so we don't want anyone else keeling over." Then he added, "They're killing us, guys."

From all the sad eyes that looked up at the coach, Michael knew what everyone felt: *We don't need someone to tell us that.*

"They have been using their speed to get us into a back-and-forth game. We've tried slowing it down to get control, but that's not working."

"They're a brick wall in front of their own goal," said Walt.

Coach held out his hand, palm up. "Here's what we're going to do. They're going to go into their shell this period and protect that four-goal lead. I want our fastest legs out there a lot. Got that, Jordan? I want you on point every other shift — I'd have you out every shift if you could do it. I want you breaking for the goal at every opportunity. We are all depending on Jordan and his speed. Got it?"

Coach paused to make sure they had.

Suddenly Vince's voice was raised. "Coach, you need to use Michael more."

16 Provincial Champs

Coach looked Vince in the eye and smiled, like they were sharing a joke.

"But Michael's been out there," he said. "He's had his shifts."

"He should be on a regular shift," said Vince. "Put him on with me."

Coach laughed. "Who's the coach here, by the way?"

"Sorry, sir," Vince continued. "But I think yesterday he showed he could do it."

Coach shook his head. "You think he can stick to that stringbean Abrams?" He turned to Michael. "Do you?"

Michael searched for words and found none.

"He can run, coach," Jason piped up. "Yesterday, when we were looking for you, we ran back here from the hotel."

"Jason and Vince couldn't keep up with him," said Dylan. "You should have seen it. I couldn't believe it."

"He outran both of you?" Coach asked Vince and Jason.

"And everybody else," added Dylan.

"And I've played against him, remember?" added Vince. "I've seen what he can do."

Coach Vickers stroked his chin. "If *you guys* are convinced Michael can do it, and Michael is convinced, that's good enough for me."

Michael looked at Vince, then Jason, Jordan, and the rest of the team. Yes, he could do it. Or he would get flattened trying. If the guys on the team believed he could do it, he'd try to find a way.

"So, Michael," Coach asked, "are you willing to use your speed and size?"

Several players, including Michael, giggled. "I don't have much size," Michael replied, grinning.

The coach continued. "But that's the point. You as point. We want you to use your speed to look for breaks. Your size makes you hard to hit. If you can't score, create a play that will. Are you up to that?"

Michael nodded.

"We're counting on you," said the coach.

The clock showed one minute left in the break.

The coach signalled for the team to stand. "We're counting on each of you," the coach said. "You are the Thunder!"

The players used the butt end of their sticks against the board to create a rolling thunder.

"Again, do the Warriors deserve to be champs?"
yelled the coach.

"No!"

"Again!"

"*No!*"

"Who deserves to be champs?"

"Thunder!"

"Who deserves to be champs?"

"*Thunder!*"

"Who deserves to be champs?"

"*Thunder!*" thundered the Thunder

***

The first shift, Coach Vickers sent Jason and Michael
on together.

"Take turns at point," he said. "Rotate positions to
mess up their zone coverage. Keep them on their toes.
We've seen their ball control, so we'll have to try to
push them."

The Warriors gained possession first, but the strong
wall in front of Duncan kept them from the scoreboard. A wild shot bounced off the end boards and
Thunder scooped it up.

Immediately, Jordan sprinted to the attack zone,
taking up residence between two faceoff circles. Duncan fed a pass to Kevin, who fed a long hard pass to

Jason. The defenders were on Jordan like mustard on a hot dog. Michael thought that Jordan had snagged the pass, but the Warriors corners squeezed him hard.

Michael joined the attack, sprinting in from the left. When Jordan lost the ball, Michael dove into the scramble. The ball soared once overhead, bounced from the floor. Michael grabbed it on the run and flung a screened shot low and hard into the Warriors goal.

4–1.

Michael high-fived Jason and his other teammates.

"Way to go, Squirt," Vince said.

"Good effort," called the Coach. "Those legs are beginning to work."

On the floor, Jason kept his edge, playing on the high side of centre, drawing one defender to him at all times, sometimes two.

Michael watched as Duncan scooped a loose ball and head-manned it to Jason, far beyond centre. Jason grabbed the ball on first bounce, roared around the one Warriors defender near him, and broke in on the Warriors goal.

The goal made it 4–2.

"We got 'em now!" shouted Jack from the bench.

"Don't count chickens before the eggs are laid," replied Coach Vickers.

The next play, Duncan again got a quick long pass off to Jason.

But Abrams anticipated it. He soared in from the

left, intercepted the pass, and caught the Thunder defence standing idle at the sides.

5–2.

Jason came to the bench and threw his stick down in disgust. "That sucks!" he said, kicking at the bench.

"No more of that," said the coach, calmly but with an edge in his voice. "You can boot yourself if we lose, if you want. But right now I need everybody focused on what needs to be done, not what was done."

Michael had never heard Coach sound so intense. "Michael, you take the faceoff. They'll likely play Abrams, and you seem to have his number. And for all of you: forget positional play. Everything is now man-to-man. Everywhere your opponent goes, you go. Stick like glue. Take this shift with Vince, Jordan, Jack, and Kevin."

At centre, Michael took position for the faceoff. The coach had been right — it was Abrams he squared off against. All game, Michael had been watching the faceoffs — how Abrams won most by using his long reach to keep the opposing player off-balance, and then kicking or scooping the ball to a teammate. Michael saw lacrosse faceoffs as being like the game of Rock, Paper, Scissors, but instead with Clamp, Jump, Push. And Abrams, he had noted, almost always used Jump — rather than clamp the ball with the netting of his stick, he would trap it with the head of his stick.

And Jason, Michael had noticed, almost always

tried to clamp the ball. As a result he lost most faceoffs against Abrams.

Waiting for the ref's whistle, Michael tensed. He kept his balance on his feet, as the coach had taught him, and not on his hands.

At the whistle, Michael tilted the top sidewall of his stick's head back toward himself. At the same time, he pushed the head forward. This pushed the ball forward so it ended up behind Abrams. With a quick flick of his toe, Michael nudged the ball out toward Vince, who scooped it up and dodged the flailing Warriors.

Michael headed straight into the attack zone to take up a spot directly in front of the crease. He dodged back and forth, trying to block the goalie's view. The two corner defenders kept shoving, pushing, moving him out of the way. But it took the two of them to do it. He found that his quick movements caused some confusion with the defenders. If two Warriors covered him, then someone else on his team was free of a check.

Plunk, plunk, plunk. The cross-checks hit on his chest, arm, and back.

Michael spun, jumped, and dodged, avoiding the hits as much as he could, trying to keep an eye on the ball. The area in front of the goal was a war zone, the defenders pushing, shoving, cross-checking — anything to keep attackers out.

The confusion worked. Vince came in hard,

shooting from between the faceoff circles. It was a hard shot that came from up high but caught the net low on the goalie's stick side. With Michael and the wall formation of four defenders tangled and bobbing in front of him, the goalie had not even seen the shot.

5–3.

Coach Vickers signalled for Michael to stay on for the following faceoff.

Again he squared off with Abrams. The two tensed at centre, muscles quivering, awaiting the whistle.

"Goose grease on the ball," Michael said.

Abrams started to laugh just as the ref's whistle sounded. Michael clamped down hard. Abrams, anticipating the jump move that had beaten him the time before, pushed.

Michael used his body and shorter legs to push Abrams off the ball. Then he scooped the ball and spun in reverse, dodging once before passing quickly to Dylan.

Dylan headed deep, cut in toward the goal, and shot hard waist high, bouncing the ball off the goalpost on the far side.

The ball bounced back out to Jack coming in on the far side. Since the shot had hit the goalpost, the shot clock was reset. This gave the Thunder possession, and another thirty seconds to shoot.

Jack roared in hard, trying to take advantage of the reeling goalie. He faked a quick shot, then finessed a pass to Michael, who passed again to Dylan. Dylan relayed the pass into the corner of the goal from just outside the crease.

5–4.

In the stands, the Thunder fans yelled, "Ooogga, Ooogga, Ooogga!"

"Boogga, Boogga, Boogga!"

"Thunder, Thunder, Thunder!"

Michael glanced over to see his own dad in a group of fathers. They were lined up on the outside of the boards, using their feet on the boards for a rumble that rocked the arena.

"Thunder, Thunder, Thunder!"

Duncan retrieved the ball and passed quickly to Jordan, who in turn caught Michael with a high hard pass just over centre. In a burst of speed, Michael split between the last two defenders and went in alone to score.

5–5. Tie game.

The crowd exploded. At the bench, Coach Vickers pointed to a diagram on his clipboard. "Michael, you're doing well on the faceoffs. Keep it up. And that long pass is working. But now they'll expect it. So let's fool them."

"Sir?"

"Hint that you might be going long, just to keep them on their toes. Then make sure you're back to take out the shooting lane."

"Right."

Michael took the faceoff against Abrams.

This time, Abrams came down hard on the whistle. But Michael pulled his stick up in a jump move, trapping Abrams' stick under his. He pulled the ball out quickly and rolled a pass to Jordan.

Michael looked at the shot clock — twenty-five seconds. The game clock showed less than a minute to go. The last thing they wanted was for the Warriors to end up with possession for the last thirty seconds. He streaked straight down centre, while Jordan roared down the right side.

Jordan saw Michael's intent, and tried to cut in from the angle. But Warriors defenders blocked his way, and his shot was not hard, accurate, or on goal. The ball bounced into the corner where the Warriors scooped it up for possession.

Rather than race back to join his team in a defensive wall in front of Duncan, Michael chased after the Warriors corner who had the ball, hounding him repeatedly, using his speed to stay with him as he moved down the floor.

His effort slowed down the Warriors' progress, but didn't stop it. Michael kept after his check even when they reached his own defensive zone.

The Warriors passed the ball once, twice, looking for an opening, knowing that this might be their last chance before overtime to score.

Thud, thud. Michael continued to pummel his check. With one last glance at the shot clock, the

Warrior shooter finally fired a hard desperation shot into the row of defenders at a goal he could not see.

Jack caught the rebound off the backboards. Both Michael and Jordan streaked toward the Warriors goal. Quickly, Jack fired off a pass with more hope than aim.

But now there were two Thunder players on the attack, and one Warriors defender. The ball bounced loosely down the court. Michael's speed had brought him into the attack zone. The goalie, who had started to the corner to retrieve the ball, changed his mind. Jason scooped up the ball on a bounce out of the corner and passed quickly to Michael on the opposite faceoff circle.

Michael waggled his stick once and fired a high hard shot into the near corner of the goal.

6–5. The Thunder was ahead!

In the stands, Michael's father was on his feet, arms overhead, his voice clear.

"Thunder! Thunder! Thunder!"

Twenty-nine seconds to go.

The Warriors called a time out.

"We'll be short," said Coach Vickers, as the team gathered around the bench. "The faceoff is the key. Whatever we do, we want possession. We don't want to give them a chance to tie it up."

He looked at the eager faces in front of him.

"Jason."

"Yes, sir?"

"Sit this one out. We need Michael's speed out there. Kevin, left crease. Jack, left corner. Vince, right corner."

A pause.

"Michael, you take the faceoff. They'll likely play Abrams."

At centre, Michael took position for the faceoff. The coach had been right — it was Abrams he squared off against.

Rock, Paper, Scissors. Rock breaks scissors, scissors cut paper, paper covers rock. Clamp, Jump, Push.

Which should Michael use? He didn't really know.

But when the whistle blew, he clamped down on the ball. He had beaten Abrams with this move before, but gambled that he would not be expecting him to repeat it.

But Abrams pushed forward and, in a quick grabbing motion, hooked his fingers on Michael's stick. It was an illegal move that Michael had only read about. By the time he realized what had happened, Abrams stood against the boards with his back to him, the ball safely nestled in the webbing of his stick.

Out of nowhere, Brandon flew in with a hard well-aimed cross check that splattered Abrams into the boards.

The ref's whistle was shrill and fast. The signal: hitting from behind. Two-minute penalty to the Thunder. A glance at the clock told the story: twenty-five seconds to go.

Out of the corner of his eye, Michael could see the Warriors goalie headed for the bench. Not only was the Thunder a man short, but the Warriors had an extra runner: six Warriors attackers against four Thunder defenders and Duncan. With possession to the Warriors.

All the Warriors needed was one clean chance for a shot on goal. And twenty seconds or so to create it.

Michael rushed to join his teammates in a defensive wall in front of their goal.

The Warriors came on strong, the sixth player joining the attack. Michael and his teammates shifted their positions to keep the attack at bay. The Warriors used sharp fast passes, probing for a weak spot.

Zing! Zang! Zop!

Michael could hear the passes singing into the webbing of the sticks. At one point Abrams took a pass. Michael covered the space between him and the goal. Robbed of what could have been a good chance, Abrams passed instead.

Ten seconds.

The Warriors sixth player took a pass at the top of the faceoff circle. A powerfully built player, he powered in as though he would carve an opening to the goal if he could not find one.

Michael saw him coming and headed straight for him.

Head down, stick gripped firmly across his chest,

137

Michael blocked the path of the charging attacker. The attacker, a head taller than Michael and several kilos heavier, pressed in.

They collided with a heavy thud that put Michael on his back, counting the rivets in the girders over his head. His head felt like it was in an echo chamber.

But the Warriors attacker fell, too, and the ball dribbled lamely into the corner.

Around Michael, cheers went up — cheers of joy, cheers of winning.

"Ooogga, Ooogga, Ooogga!"

"Boogga, Boogga, Boogga!"

"Thunder, Thunder, Thunder!"

For a moment he could not move.

He struggled to one elbow, slipped, then struggled up on his wobbly feet.

The buzzer sounded.

Michael was in the middle of a pile of players — happy victorious players.

"We won!" Duncan said, hugging him firmly. "We won!"

Jason high-fived him. "Great block, Reilly," he said. "How's your head?"

Michael was back at the bench before his head cleared enough to realize what the team had just accomplished. The Thunder were provincial champs.

17 A New Player

In the parking lot after the game, they all celebrated under the canopy behind Coach Vickers' van — the Thunder, their parents, some siblings.

And Michael's father.

"Wow!" said Rebekah, charging up to Michael as his family arrived. "That was great! You are a hero."

Michael laughed. "Don't let the guys hear you say things like that."

Jason snapped the top of a can of soda pop. "That was some shot you took to the head," he said to Michael. "And to think, I didn't think you were stupid enough to block a shot."

"Small, fast, but mighty," said Coach Vickers. "That's Michael."

Michael was surprised when Scotty Martin appeared at their victory party. "I just wanted to congratulate the Thunder on a great tournament," Mr. Martin said. "You beat a very good team today. Maybe

I'll be seeing some of you guys at the national level some day."

To Michael he said, "I like your persistence. That's one of the things I look for when I'm putting together a team. A team isn't the stars. The quality of a team rests with the guys who made the team and spend most of their time on the bench."

"Not that Michael will be doing that now," said Coach Vickers.

Finally, Michael was walking across the parking lot with his family around him.

"I'm glad you made it to this game," said Michael.

"Me, too," said his father. "I wouldn't miss seeing that for the world."

"That was a super goal you scored," said his mother.

"Which one?" said Rebekah. "I counted three that Michael scored!"

Mrs. Reilly took Rebekah by the hand. "Oh, Bekah, where did you leave your dolls this time? Are they back in the arena?"

Rebekah shook her head from side to side. "I did-n't bring them, remember? They're back in the hotel. In my suitcase."

"Oh, Honeybun, you are growing up."

"Mom? Dad?" said Rebekah. "Can I get a lacrosse stick?"

"A lacrosse …?" asked her father.

"Yes. A lacrosse stick."

"Whatever for?"

Rebekah showed her gap-toothed grin. "Next year, I want to play lacrosse," she said proudly. "I want to be a hero like my brother."

Box Lacrosse Basics

Box lacrosse is played in a hockey rink with no ice. Teams are made up of six players: a goalie, left crease, right crease, point, left corner (or shooter), and right corner (or shooter). Left and right crease are in some ways similar to left and right wing in hockey; the point is similar to the centre: and the corners (or shooters) are similar to defence in hockey.

In box lacrosse, there is no off-side. In this respect the game is like basketball. The rule allows a team to pass the full length of the box, or pass to a player near the opponents goal.

Cross-checking is legal. Any member of the team in possession of the ball may be checked. A cross-check may not be delivered from behind or to force the opponent into the boards. The player in possession of the ball who uses a free hand or arm to ward off a check will be penalized.

Play stops when a shot hits the goalie in the helmet or face mask. Possession is given to the goalie. Any player (or a goalie out of the crease) who grabs the ball in the hand will be penalized. Kicking the ball is allowed, but goals scored by kicking are not allowed. The goalie with possession of the ball in the goal crease has five seconds to pass the ball. A team serving a penalty has ten seconds to advance the ball beyond centre. The usual thirty-second rule for shooting on the opponent's goal still applies.

Some Lacrosse Terms

Cross-check: Hitting the opponent with a stick held in two hands. Contact with the opponent must be between the shoulders and the knees, and only with the portion of the stick held between the hands. This is legal if the opposing team has possession.

Deke: To move quickly from side to side with faking motions to avoid a check. Originally a hockey term, this applies to lacrosse as well.

Shot clock: A digital clock at each end of the arena counts down from thirty seconds each time a team gains possession of the ball.

Faceoff: The faceoff is held with sticks on the floor and the open part of the stick (webbing) facing the player's own goal. The ball must come out of the 2-foot faceoff circle before it can be touched by other players.

Man-to-man: The defending team plays each player against a specific opponent instead of defending a defined zone in front of the goal.

Positional play: When defending in front of their own goal, most teams will assign players to cover a specific area in front of the goal.